Rainwater Kisses

A Billionaire Love Story

KRISTA LAKES

ISBN-13: **978-1-948467-13-1**

*To my little sister.
I love you.*

ACKNOWLEDGMENTS

A special thank you to everyone involved in this amazing process. You know who you are and that I am eternally grateful.

I would especially like to thank my editor and husband. Without the two of you, who knows what the comma situation would have looked like!

CHAPTER ONE

Emma laughed gently and touched Jack Saunders' shoulder. He smiled and seemed to unconsciously reach for her hand, the two of them leaning closer to one another. They looked so happy together, so perfectly in love that it was impossible to look at them without feeling their happiness. Jack leaned over and whispered something into Emma's ear. She blushed and giggled before reaching for her wine glass.

Emma looked radiant. I didn't know if I'd ever seen my little sister look so happy, and that happiness was translating into an inner beauty that shone out across the whole ocean. People on the other side of the world were probably wondering what was making that joyful glow. Jack matched her elation in a masculine way, his sandy hair blowing softly in the Caribbean wind as we finished the last of our dinners. They were the perfect couple.

The entire wedding party for Jack and Emma sat outdoors at a large wooden dinner table, the evening breeze blowing warmly. If the wedding dinner was anywhere near as fancy as this rehearsal dinner was, I would gain at least five pounds on this trip.

I typically didn't like traveling. In fact, I never traveled. I had never even left the Midwest, but I thought that this ocean breeze was something I could definitely get used to.

Jack and Emma sat at the head of the big square table as if they were the king and queen of the tropical island. I sat next to Emma with my parents on the other side of me. Across the table was Jack's best man, Owen. Down the line sat his younger brother, mother and father.

We were all gathered to celebrate the marriage of Jack to my little sister, Emma. Jack had flown the whole family, plus friends, out to an island in the Caribbean for the ceremony and paid for a week at the island resort for everyone. I had only been able to get four days off from my job at the hospital, and now I wished I had more in this beautiful place. I wasn't sure exactly what this trip had cost, but I knew it was far above what my paycheck could afford. Of course, for him it was no big deal. He could afford to do this because he was the President and CEO of DS Oil and Gas. He was a billionaire, after all.

The two of them were getting married on the

very island where they met, on the very beach where Emma had saved a man's life while Jack kept cool next to her. This time, though, it was for real. For some wild reason, when they first met, they had decided to get married, despite hardly knowing one another. Emma said it was a crazy, spur-of-the-moment vacation memory thing, but I still thought she was insane. It wasn't a legal wedding, of course. They were outside of the US and there were no papers signed.

It should have ended there, except that the paparazzi happened to somehow get some pictures of their wedding and posted them everywhere. I actually found out my sister was married by reading the tabloid headlines at the grocery store. It had been the first time I ever actually bought one of those magazines. Before I could even talk to her, however, she had zipped off to New York City so that Jack could do damage control.

It took a while for the press to die down enough for her to come back to Iowa. By then, it was pretty apparent that she and Jack were a sure thing. Emma and I had some rather personal conversations, and I found myself marveling at my little sister. The things she was willing to put up with, particularly Jack's work schedule, were things that I wouldn't have tolerated. She loved him though, and she was willing to deal with it. He finally proposed over Christmas dinner. Now, here we were on the island for a beautiful spring wedding.

I was actually supposed to have gone on the vacation that started it all. Emma had won a trip for two from the local radio station, but I came down with appendicitis two days before the flight. During the week that she spent in the Caribbean, I spent my time hopped up on painkillers and antibiotics, and thinking that I was the one going to do crazy things. Sitting here, though, watching the two of them be so obviously in love, made me glad I hadn't come. My little sister deserved this kind of happiness.

I looked across the table and Owen was staring at me. As soon as we made eye contact, he grinned. My cheeks turned red and I quickly looked away. I hadn't had a chance to really speak with him yet since he had arrived late in the afternoon, just in time for the practice walk down the aisle.

He had sauntered up to the wedding area, breezing past the security guards and personal assistants with an easy familiarity. Emma introduced us in the moment before the wedding planner took control and started directing everyone to their places. He had held my hand for a split second longer than necessary when he shook it, as if he were reluctant to let go. From that moment on, he had flirted with me mercilessly.

Owen Parker. Probably the most gorgeous man I had ever met. Blonde hair that fell in perfect Disney hero fashion, dark blue eyes, and a jaw that could cut steel, not to mention the way he filled out a suit. He looked like he belonged on the cover of a romance novel, and the way he smiled at me only reinforced that impression.

Like Jack, Owen was also fabulously wealthy. He made more in a day working at Jack's company than I did in a year as a physician's assistant. Not only that, he came from old money, and he had been very wise with his investments over the years. I knew he was one of the few people that Jack trusted, because Jack knew that he had no interest in his money. In fact, the only reason he had this job was because it was a challenge to him; the money was just a perk.

Jack and Owen had been college roommates, and the friendship was an easy thing between them. I could only imagine what kind of trouble the two of them had gotten into in college. They probably broke a lot of girls' hearts

It was clear to see that Owen came from a lifetime of privilege and money. The way he nonchalantly ordered a thousand-dollar bottle of wine, used all the forks and spoons correctly, and the lack of concern for his expensive clothing all made it obvious to me that he had more money than he could ever spend.

During the entire rehearsal, he had kept grinning at me and mimicking the planner when she wasn't looking, forcing the rest of the wedding party to stifle our laughs. I wanted to like him, but something about his charm was too easy. I knew he could have any woman he wanted and that he was used to women falling in love with him. With how flirtatious he was being, I could make this my own vacation to remember if I wanted. . However, it was too easy for the best man and the maid of honor to hook up at a wedding, and I didn't want to be a cliché conquest.

I was trying my best to ignore him, but it was difficult.

Mr. Daniel Saunders, Jack's father, tapped his wine glass with a knife, sending a crystal ping for silence across the table. Everyone at the table quickly quieted as he stood slowly, the motion obviously taking more energy than expected, but he did his best. He lifted his glass in a toast.

"I would like to congratulate my son... and welcome Emma as a daughter." As quiet as he was, even with the noticeable pause in the sentence, his voice was still full of authority. Despite his evident physical weakness, he still held the power of a billionaire oil baron. He paused, taking a shallow breath, and the glass wavered in the air as his arm lost the strength to hold it. Mrs. Saunders stood up quickly beside him, wrapping her arm around him as though she were hugging him, but supporting him and his shaking arm in the process.

"We are glad to welcome you into the family," Mrs. Saunders continued for him, and Mr. Saunders gave her a grateful look. To a casual observer it appeared as though they were simply a loving couple, but I could see Mrs. Saunders' muscles tighten as she kept him upright.

"At first, I wasn't sure that this life would be what you wanted, Emma. But, the past few months have shown me that this is what you were born to do. The two of you make an unstoppable team and I can't remember the last time I saw my Jack this happy. Daniel and I are proud to welcome you to the family," Mrs Saunders said, flashing a smile around the table. Mr. Saunders smiled weakly, but with obvious joy as he slowly attempted to lift his glass.

I raised my own glass with a tip to the Saunders and took a sip of wine. It was a sweet white with just enough bubbles to tickle my nose. I pretended to look at the liquid in the glass, but I was really looking at Mr. Saunders. His suit was tailored perfectly, but it couldn't hide the tell-tale signs that he was losing the battle against his cancer. Despite the fine fabric, it hung off of him as though he were made of nothing but bones. I had seen enough patients come into the ER to know that this was going to be his last wedding. The tabloids were full of stories of advanced cancer, and from what I could see, it was a good thing Emma and Jack were getting married when they were. I wouldn't expect him to last more than a month at this point.

Mrs. Saunders helped her husband sit back down in his wheelchair, the white in her knuckles betraying the amount of strength she had to use as his legs gave out. I shook my head slightly and looked at Emma and Jack. Jack didn't seem to notice, or was doing a very good job of hiding his emotions. Emma smiled at the older man and he gave her a grin in return. She got along better with Mr. Saunders than she did with Mrs. Saunders. Despite Mrs. Saunders' kind toast, Emma had told me that she still felt like Mrs. Saunders was just waiting for Jack to grow bored with her. She was always polite, but Emma knew that she was never going to be the favorite daughter-in-law.

Life couldn't be that perfect, I thought.

"Well, I suppose now is the time for speeches. I have an exciting and dramatic one planned for tomorrow, but an impromptu one is called for today," said Owen, rising gracefully. He made the simple motion of rising somehow look choreographed and elegant. He instantly captured the attention of every eye at the dinner, and he flashed a handsome grin around the table.

"First, a word for Emma. I know that Jack has some bad habits. I was his housemate in college, and despite having the best staff in the building, I still found his dirty socks all over the floor. He also snores, forgets to put the lid down, and has a tendency to take everything far too seriously."

Owen paused for a moment and Jack called out, "Gee, thanks buddy."

"I saw a lot of girls come and go. I've seen him with supermodels, heiresses, lingerie models, and even once, a secretary." Emma frowned slightly, but Owen smiled, promising a compliment in the end. "But, I never saw him with a girl as beautiful, or a girl that made him as happy as you do. The two of you fit together like you were made for one another, and I couldn't be more happy for you both."

Emma smiled and Jack squeezed her hand. Owen turned slightly to face Jack.

"For Jack, you have something most of us can only dream of. You have a beautiful woman who puts up with the strange situations that our careers put us in. A woman who, somehow, has found a way to flourish within it. Hold onto her. The two of you have a beautiful future ahead. That being said, if you ever need a break from him, Emma, you know where to find me." Owen ended his speech with a suggestive wink and a raise of his glass.

Everyone at the table clapped loudly and laughed as Emma blushed slightly at the offer. Jack chuckled and kissed Emma's cheek, making her smile. I felt a slight stab of envy as my sister lit up. I was the older sister, but my little sister was about to get married and I didn't even have a date for the wedding. I immediately chided myself for feeling jealous. I loved that she was happy and so thoroughly in love. She deserved every moment of joy and prosperity.

Jack's little brother Robbie stood up once it was quiet.

"Jack, let me thank you again for not making me the best man," he started. His words were slurring just a little bit. "I would have lost the ring, been late, and there is no way I could come up with a good speech. Besides, Owen will look prettier in the pictures. I am really glad to be here, though, and I'm even more glad that it's because my older brother is marrying someone as awesome as Emma. Emma, you are the sister I never had, and I am excited to get to call you family. That's it. Kanpai!" The Japanese toast hung in the air as he slammed back the last of his wine and sat down, motioning to the waiter for more.

My father glanced around and then stood, raising his glass as well. "I guess it's my turn," he said.

He looked down at his youngest daughter.

"Emma, you will always be my little girl. I am so proud that you have found your way in the world. I want you to know that your mother and I are so very proud of you." My dad's eyes grew blurry as he continued, unable to hide the waver of emotion running through his voice. I knew this was hard for him. Emma was the baby of the family.

"Jack, I know you are going to take good care of our baby. I'm proud to finally have a son in the family. Cheers!" Everyone sipped their drink and gave a light applause.

I waited for the applause to die down before I stood up. "I guess that makes it my turn. Jack, you treat my sister the way she deserves to be treated-like a princess. I know you make her happy, because she has this glow that she only gets around you. I've never seen her so happy or so sure of herself. Thank you." Jack tipped his head in acknowledgment and smiled. I turned toward Emma.

"Em, when Mom and Dad brought you home, I said I wanted a puppy instead. I still want the dog, but, today, I'm glad I've got you. I love you, Sis. Thank you for letting me be a part of this." I had intended to say more, but my voice caught and I didn't trust myself not to cry. It didn't help that Emma looked about ready to cry too. She jumped up and immediately gave me a hug.

"Thanks, KayKay," she whispered into my ear. I wiped a tear off my cheek and tried to look at the sky to make the rest of the tears go back to where they came from as I let her go. She grinned at me as she sat down, her eyes shining too.

As everyone settled, a well-dressed waiter came and whispered into Jack's ear. Jack laughed and shook his head, looking over at Emma.

"For once it isn't one of my phone calls that is urgently interrupting." The waiter handed Emma a message. She read it quickly, and then smiled apologetically at the table.

"Excuse me for just a minute. They can't seem to function without me anymore." She stood, kissed Jack on the cheek, and ducked into the main building. Through the window, I could see her pick up a phone.

I wondered what could be so important that anyone would interrupt her wedding rehearsal dinner. Since officially moving to New York, Emma had found a way to merge her dreams of working with animals and living with Jack. She had wanted to be a veterinarian since we were kids, but if she wanted to be with Jack, that wouldn't be possible. Every patient would know she had infinitely deep pockets and would always be looking for a way to get free care or sue for any mistake, no matter how minor.

But, Emma being Emma, she had found a way.

She created the "Daniel Saunders Wildlife and Marine Rehabilitation Program" through Jack's company using their environmental restoration department. Everyday, she was able to work with Jack and with rehabilitating animals. She loved it, and it had been a good way to honor Jack's father, but it kept her as busy as Jack. Honestly though, I couldn't see her any other way. Emma was just too hard a worker to stop just because she got married.

Emma came back out the door, her light blue dress trailing after her in the evening breeze. She smiled at Jack and sat down to finish her wine, the phone call finished. Jack smiled with obvious pride at his soon-to-be-legally-married wife. The table was quiet, everyone sipping on the last of their wine and enjoying the evening.

"Thank you for a lovely evening, but it is time for us to retire," Mrs. Saunders said as Emma sat down. She rose and stood behind Mr. Saunders' chair. The old man was struggling to keep his eyes open, seemingly exhausted by the dinner and toast. Emma jumped up and gave Mrs. Saunders a friendly hug. She was determined to win Jack's mother over eventually. Mrs. Saunders returned the affection and Emma bent to give Mr. Saunders a kiss on the cheek. He beamed up at her, and waved as Jack's assistant, Rachel, wheeled his chair away. The table watched quietly as they disappeared around a perfectly manicured hedge and into the deepening night.

"I think we'll hit the hay too," my dad said as he pushed his chair out. He stood and shook Jack's hand before giving Emma a kiss. Mom gave them both a hug, her eyes bright. Her baby girl was getting married, and she was so incredibly proud and excited. She kissed my head as she walked past. I watched my parents walk hand and hand down the stone path, still very much in love. I hoped to find a love like theirs someday.

"I think that leaves just us young-uns," Jack's little brother said with a grin. "Bring on the tequila!"

"Sorry, Robbie, I have an early morning," Jack said. "Technically so do you, but since you just have to stand there and look pretty, it shouldn't be too hard." He leaned back in his chair, in no obvious hurry to get anywhere.

"What about the amazing bachelor party I have planned?" Robbie asked with mock seriousness.

Jack grimaced and Emma laughed. From what I had heard, the New York bachelor party had been a crazy enough party for Jack. He wouldn't say exactly what they did, but he had refused to drink anything besides water and Gatorade for a week.

"What about you, Kaylee?" Owen asked. He said my name slowly, as though he liked the way it felt on his lips. To be honest, I liked the way it sounded coming out of his mouth, but I was not about to do anything to encourage him.

I shrugged. "I'll probably have an early night. We have a busy day tomorrow."

Owen nodded, his blue eyes intent on mine. "Perhaps I can interest you in a drink before you go?"

I opened my mouth, but nothing came out. I wanted to say no, but it was as if he was hypnotizing me to say yes. The way he held his body, his eyes catching mine and the seductive tone of voice, it was all incredibly hard to say no to. No wonder the guy was a marketing VP.

"Count me in!" Robbie said with a smirk before I

could actually answer. Owen gave him a sideways glare. The spell was broken.

"You oversold it. Even I was tempted," Jack said, finishing his drink. Owen gave him a dirty look to match the one he had shot Robbie.

"If I wasn't marrying this handsome man tomorrow, I would have been all over that," Emma said and smiled sweetly at him. Owen raised his hands in defeat. It was easy to tell that his method of picking up women was a known thing among the four of them.

"Fine, too obvious. Question still stands though Kaylee. Would you like to get a drink?" Owen asked, his smile hopeful. I had to nip this in the bud before he could try that hypnotizing look again. Girls probably fell for him left and right with that smolder.

"Sorry, no. I've sworn off men for a little while," I said. I did not want to get burned by a man like I did last time. "Especially men who buy me drinks."

Possibly forever, I thought.

Owen tipped his chin down and gave me the biggest blue puppy eyes I have ever seen. I'm not sure quite how he did it, but it took a lot of willpower not to give in. When he started to tremble his lower lip, I almost caved, but then Jack started to laugh.

"Oh Kaylee, I think he likes you! He never does the puppy thing unless he's desperate," Jack just barely managed to say before he began to laugh. He and Emma were both snorting into their wine at the pathetic face Owen was making.

"You guys are seriously ruining my mojo. This works every time." Owen glared at the happy couple, sparing an angry glance for Robbie, who was cracking up in the corner.

"I think I'm going to go to bed," I said, knowing full well those blue eyes would get me if I stayed. I needed to avoid men for a little while for my own good. Owen smiled up at me as I stood from the table.

"Would you like me to join you?" he asked. He practically oozed charm. It wasn't a bad thing. In fact, it was rather nice to be so obviously desired, but I had no interest in a random hookup. I wasn't looking for a good time, and I certainly wasn't looking for a relationship. Not that he was even offering the latter.

"You are persistent! Thanks, but no thanks," I said, shaking my head. I gave Emma a hug and Jack surprised me with a hug from him. I was liking Jack more and more.

"You sure? I give excellent back rubs," Owen tried again. I knew he was just playing so I pretended to think about it, holding a finger up to my lips.

"Hmm... nope."

"Break my heart!" he cried, falling back into his chair as though I had wounded him. He grinned and gave me a wink as I made sure I had my room key. Robbie came around the table and gave me a big bear hug, practically lifting me off the floor.

"Have a great night, Kaylee," Robbie said with a grin before turning to Owen and adding, "and that's how you do it."

"Well, if that's how it's done," Owen said, rising gracefully. He stepped close to me and my heart started pounding in my chest for no apparent reason. I had told myself I wasn't going to give into him, and I was going to stick by it, no matter how much he made my insides heat.

"Have a wonderful night, Kaylee. Dream sweet," he whispered as he wrapped me up in his arms. For one glorious second, I let myself imagine being his. My body ached to be touched, to be wrapped up with his. His cologne was masculine but not overpowering, his arms strong and confident around me. I honestly didn't want him to let go, but he released me before it could even be considered awkward. I hoped I wasn't blushing too noticeably.

"You all have a good night," I managed to stutter before heading down the stone pathway off the porch. I stepped into the twilight, feeling the warm tropical evening surround me. The waves shushed in the distance and night insects sang in the bushes while the stars twinkled above. It was something that I would have typically enjoyed, but right then, all I could think about was how good Owen had smelled.

CHAPTER TWO

I watched as my dad walked my little sister down the aisle. Or rather, down the beach we had made into an aisle. Dad kissed her softly before reluctantly letting go. Jack grinned like the happiest person in the world as she stepped towards him.

Emma was stunning. She wore a flowing white dress that billowed slightly in the breeze and was just formal enough for a wedding, but casual enough that it screamed Emma. Her long dark hair was half up in a complicated series of braids. and the rest blew softly in the gentle wind. She chose not to go with a veil, instead having tiny white flowers that matched her bouquet sprinkled throughout the dark braids. She looked like something out of a fairytale which, considering the man she was marrying, was appropriate.

She handed me her flowers and turned to face Jack. Everything about her was glowing. Her happiness was infectious. I couldn't have wiped the smile off my face if I tried. The minister began in a deep voice, the audience sitting with rapt attention. My mother kept dotting her eyes, tears of joy spilling down her face.

"Do you, Emma LaRue, take this man to be your lawfully wedded husband? To have and to hold, in sickness and in health, for richer or poorer, for better or for worse, for as long as you both shall live?"

Emma's voice shook slightly as she answered, "I do." I knew she was happy, her entire being vibrating with joy. Jack grinned as she promised herself to him, a boyish enthusiasm radiating out from him in waves.

I really liked Jack. I hadn't gotten to spend much time with him up until now, as he was often busy with the job of heading a major oil company. The transition of leadership from the elderly Daniel Saunders leading the company to the younger Jack Saunders had been stressful, but he seemed to overflow with confidence now. Emma and I had discussed how swamped he had been, and how that meant she didn't get to see him as much as she would have liked. She had been overjoyed when the transition period ended and he was able to leave work every night to be with her.

The fact that Jack adored my little sister made him a good guy in my book. Every time she walked into the room, his eyes followed her, gleaming with love, and that told me that he was head over heels for her. I loved the way she smiled and lit up whenever they were together. The money was an added bonus, but I knew she would have loved him even if he had been broke.

Jack slid a ring on her finger, the light catching on a massive diamond that cast a bright fire across the entire crowd. It was fitting, because their love burned like a fire that cast happiness across everyone they met.

Still, I hoped she wasn't going swimming later because with that rock on her hand, she would drown. Owen put the ring box back into his pocket and caught my eye. We made eye contact and he grinned at me. My skin went hot, and I looked back at the ring, flustered.

I had dreamed about him all night. *Dream sweet,* he had said, and sweet dreams I had. I tried to pay attention to the rest of the ceremony, but I could feel Owen's eyes on me. And why not? I thought. Jack's assistant had picked out a great dress for me, a strapless coral-colored dress. She had contacted a tailor out in Iowa to measure me and modify the dress to hug all my contours. I couldn't believe how good it looked on me, the color accenting my dark hair and the cut making me look like a supermodel.

I wanted to look back up at Owen, but I knew if I did, I would blush. The man was too charming for his own good. *Why is it this hard to just ignore a man?* I thought. I was lost in thought for a moment as Jack recited his vows.

"I now pronounce you husband and wife! You

may kiss the bride!"

Everyone let out a cheer as Jack leaned forward and kissed Emma. I let out a whoop and raised my bouquet to the sky, genuinely happy for my little sister. The cameras flashed and clicked as the two of them broke apart, grins plastered on their faces. Jack grabbed her hand, and together they took off down the aisle, the rest of the bridal party following at a more sedate pace.

Owen met me at the center point and offered his arm. I took it, and he grinned as he walked me down the aisle. His arm felt strong against mine, his muscles flexed as he escorted me back towards the resort. I wondered if the rest of his body would feel as nice under me.

Stop it, I thought. I had promised myself no men for a while, and no matter how good Owen looked in a suit or how much he flirted with me, I wasn't about to give in. I braced myself for the inevitable flirting that I knew I would endure as soon as the ceremony was over.

CHAPTER THREE

As the guests filed their way to the reception area, Owen continued to walk with me toward the head table. When we reached it, he pulled my chair out without a word. I smiled and nodded at him. "Thank you, sir."

"You're welcome, ma'am," he replied, a warm smile on his face. He turned and walked to his chair, waiting for the rest of the party to begin.

I smiled to myself. His overt sexuality hadn't worked, so now he had decided to be a gentleman. *I'm onto your little games, Mr. Parker,* I thought to myself. I had to admit though, it was cute.

The bride and groom stood at the entrance to the outdoor reception area, thanking each guest who came in. Jack had invited a lot more people than Emma had, and my parents still hadn't arrived at their table. I looked for someone to talk to and suddenly found myself looking in Owen's direction. He was looking right at me, smiling. I blushed and looked away quickly. *It couldn't hurt to talk to him just a little bit...*

Suddenly, the DJ's voice came over the speakers. Supposedly they had flown him in from New York as well, so I expected to get some dancing in later. "Alright, let's get this party started! Can I get the bride and groom on the dance floor for their first dance as a married couple?"

I watched as my sister and her husband walked to the middle of the dance floor and embrace each other as a slow song started. Both Jack and Emma were usually talented dancers, but as the music played, they just hugged each other tightly and danced as if they really had been married for a while now, instead of only a day. Their long, confusing courtship was finally over and they were able to move on with their lives.

About halfway through the song, a tired looking Daniel Saunders wheeled his way onto the dance floor. Whispers were exchanged between father and son, and Jack steadied the older man's wheelchair as Emma helped him to his feet. Emma held him delicately as they shuffled along to the music, the elderly Saunders doing his best to keep up with the slow beat but unable to shuffle fast enough. Jack stood nearby with the wheelchair, dutifully waiting for his father to finish, a sad smile on his face. Emma hugged the frail man tightly, and I saw tears in the eyes of several of the guests as they watched the man struggle.

As the song ended, Jack brought the wheelchair to Daniel. The DJ spoke up then. "Can we get all the rest of the fathers out there to dance with their daughters?" My dad moved his way out to the dance floor, but Daniel held on tightly to Emma. He leaned on his wheelchair and whispered something to Jack. Jack frowned slightly, but I saw the fire in Daniel's eyes flare up as he made a demand of some sort. Jack nodded and went to a nearby table.

There sat Rachel, Jack's personal assistant. The elderly Mr. Saunders had groomed her since joining the company to be the billionaire's right hand man. It seemed to me that she probably had the most tears on her face of everyone at the wedding. Jack extended his hand to her and she accepted it.

I watched as Dad reached Emma, allowing her to continue to support the old man until Jack returned with Rachel. Rachel wrapped her arms around his weak body and he almost fell into her, but caught himself at the last moment. Emma squeezed his hand one last time before solemnly turning to face Dad. As soon as Mr. Saunders was safely entrusted to Rachel, Emma and Dad smiled at them, then danced away.

Daniel no longer shuffled his feet, he just leaned into Rachel as other couples danced around them. Jack still stood next to the wheelchair, ready for him. I saw Daniel whisper something in Rachel's ear, and she burst out in laughter through her tears.

I was surprised that any doctor would let him travel, but I doubted he really asked permission. This was going to be his last dance, and he knew it. He would have spent all the billions of dollars of his company to be here if he had needed to.

As the song ended, I saw Dad dip Emma, then kiss her on the forehead as she came back up. They embraced each other deeply. I looked back over as Rachel eased Mr. Saunders back into the wheelchair, her small frame able to handle his skin and bones with ease. Jack rolled his father back to his table while my father walked Emma back to her table.

The music still played, but I felt like you could still hear a pin drop in the place. My dad tapped me on the shoulder. "Do you mind if I get a dance from you?" I smiled and extended my hand, and my father led me to the dance floor.

"You know, I always expected that you would be the first daughter I'd dance with like this," he said in my ear as we pivoted slowly.

I nodded. "I know." It wasn't that Emma was unattractive, but she had always been so studious, so unconcerned with boys. Sometimes I had envied the fact that no man seemed to be able to win her heart, whereas many men had managed to steal mine.

We danced until the song ended, and Dad did another slow dip for me, kissing me as he had Emma. He brought me close again. "Someday soon, Kaylee. Your prince will come." He squeezed my hand and smiled.

As I turned around, I was suddenly face-to-face with Prince Charming himself. "May I have the next dance?" Owen asked. I looked back at Dad, and he gave me a "go on" gesture. I shrugged. What harm could one slow dance do?

I felt Owen's strong hands wrap around me, one on my shoulder and one on my waist, pulling me in closer. Just as I had before, I wanted him to draw me in completely, to take me. *Stay strong,* I told myself. I danced slowly with him, trying to make eye contact, but looking away and blushing every time his blue eyes met mine.

"So you obviously know what I do. What do you do?" Owen asked finally, the plain question breaking the tension. Maybe he didn't feel any tension at all. Maybe he was just being friendly.

"I'm a physician's assistant in the ER," I said.

"So... like a secretary?" he asked.

I rolled my eyes. "Nothing like a secretary," I said, a little annoyed at the question. The song was ending, so he dipped me down low. The form fitting coral dress didn't help the fact that I felt like I was being thrown into bed, and he lingered for just a moment longer than I thought he would at the bottom of the dip. Finally he lifted me back up.

"I want to hear all about being a physician's assistant," he said.

I opened my mouth, ready to tell him everything as we began to walk back to the table. Then I remembered that he knew every trick in the book. "You're just trying to get me to talk about myself, aren't you? You think that's the key to every woman's heart."

He didn't even bat an eye. "Yes I am. Is it working?"

I paused. *He's playing with me,* I thought. "No, but now you're going to have to listen to me talk about all the gross things that happen at a hospital," I said.

He pulled my chair out for me, and I sat down. He sat down in Jack's empty chair, put his elbows on the table, his face in his palms, and leaned in. "I'm all ears," he said, sounding genuinely eager.

I sighed. "Owen..."

My tone must have said it all. Owen jumped back. "Say no more. I can tell when I have no chance of making the sale. If you don't want me to talk to you again, just let me know."

I pouted. "It's not like that..."

"So you *do* want me to talk to you?" he asked, a charming smile on his face. I couldn't help but blush and look away shyly. "Look, I'll leave you be for now. If you feel like talking later, come find me." With that, he stood up, walking towards Mr. Saunders. I knew that he'd have plenty to talk about with the businesspeople at the party, so maybe it really was better that I didn't waste his time by talking about myself.

I watched him move with the confidence of a man who knew what he wanted and usually got it. Well not today Mr. Parker. Today, not even your money could buy what you wanted.

He looked back at me, those piercing blue eyes catching me in just the right way. *Take me, I'm yours... No!* The civil war in my brain continued to rage on.

***

For the next few hours, I spoke with my parents or my sister, shooting occasional glances at Owen. Most of the time, he wasn't looking at me, but sometimes, he was. Every time our eyes met, I smiled at him.

I drank a couple cups of punch, danced with a couple of Jack's younger cousins, and enjoyed the festivities. The DJ they had flown in from New York was worth every penny. When it came time for Emma to throw the bouquet, I joined the crowd. Emma winked at me as she turned around. As she threw the bouquet behind her head, I watched it sail in a perfect arc towards me. *If this was on purpose, I thought, then she must have been practicing her behind-the-back bouquet tosses.* I held out my hands to catch the bouquet- and suddenly a young teenage girl about sixteen years old jumped up and snatched it.

The crowd cheered for the young lady, and my eyes went straight to Owen. His eyes were on me too, and I gave him my best can't-win-em-all shrug. He walked over to me, drink in hand.

"You were robbed," he said.

I smiled. "I thought you weren't going to talk to me anymore," I said, a wry smile on my face.

He shrugged. "You initiated communication, even though it was nonverbal." I laughed and he continued. "Besides, you looked bored."

I leaned in and whispered. "I feel guilty, but I am a little bored. I don't know many people here, and Emma is so busy talking to people."

He shrugged again. "You know me. Listen, Jack's brother Robbie has his racing boat parked on a marina right down the beach. Why don't we take it for a spin?"

That sounds like fun, I thought. *You really shouldn't though.* I could feel my resistance breaking down. "I should really stay here until the end of the wedding."

Owen smiled. "Jack will look for any excuse to start his wedding night as soon as possible, if you catch my drift. The best man and maid of honor leaving would be such a perfect excuse. Besides, I have to hear all about the gross stuff that happens at hospitals."

Maybe just a quick boat ride...

Owen continued. "Or, if you'd like, we can just go straight back to my cabana house," he said.

I grimaced a little. *He just lost the sale,* I thought. "You know what? I do think I'll call it a night. It was a pleasure, Owen," I said.

Owen knew he had messed up. "Of course," he said, gracefully accepting defeat. "Perhaps I'll see you tomorrow," he added, hopefully.

"Perhaps," I replied coolly, not counting on him still being interested in me tomorrow. Tomorrow I would be plain old Kaylee, small town girl from Iowa, not maid of honor at his best friend's wedding. I went and said good night to my parents and gave Emma one last hug. I left quickly, looking back one last time. Owen's eyes were on me as I left, and he raised his hand in a quick, meek wave.

When I got to my room, I took a nice bath, thinking of Owen joining me in the warm suds. I turned the air conditioning in the room down to 68 and lay down in bed, watching TV as I drifted off to sleep. Somehow, even with the room being as cool as it was, I still writhed uncomfortably in bed as I slept, the thought of the strong, rich man down at that wedding consuming my every thought.

CHAPTER FOUR

The next morning, I awoke a sweaty mess. Owen had invaded my dreams, and I had a feeling he would occupy my thoughts for the rest of the day as well. Still, I had taken my first flight on an airplane in order to be here, and I was going to make the most of this vacation. Tomorrow evening I would be back on a miserable flight to Iowa, so I might as well make some memories while I was here.

I knew that Emma would probably be exhausted from partying and everything else that goes along with a wedding night, so I just grabbed a book and headed out to the beach. It was quiet on the resort, as all the guests were sleeping off the party. A tree caught my eye as I wandered towards the water, and I went to investigate. It was a funny little tree, with bunches of beautiful five petaled flowers. I picked one blossom from a branch, and held it to my nose. It was the sweetest flower I had ever smelled. I tucked one behind my ear, feeling very pretty.

I went down to the beach, not terribly interested in finding a place to read just yet. Setting the book down on a safe patch of sand, I waded into the crystal clear ocean. The water was too warm and wonderful not to at least dip my toes in at every chance. I kicked lightly at the waves, looking down the shore. A few hundred yards away was a set of cabana houses. Jack and Emma were in one of them, the two of them staying in the same cabana where they had fallen in love.

Something else caught my attention, though. A woman's scream of terror shattered the quiet of the beach. I remembered Emma's story of saving a man's life on the beach, and I knew that it now was my responsibility to do the same. I jumped to my feet, scanning the water for signs of a woman drowning. Soon I realized that the sound wasn't coming from the water-- it was coming from above...

There, hundreds of feet in the air, a woman screamed as she was pulled behind a boat. A huge red parachute kept her airborne as she flew through the air. The only thing preventing her from flying off into the stratosphere was a tether connected to her harness and the boat.

That looks fun, I thought. *Way too dangerous, though.* As the woman soared through the sky, screaming in joy and terror, I knew that I wanted to try it. It would be the perfect vacation adventure, something to tell the girls back home. This was my vacation. I had spent my whole life playing it safe, never leaving the security of Iowa. Now that I was in a faraway place, I was going to try some new things.

I turned around and picked up my book from where I left in in the sand. When I stood back up and turned around, I was face to face with Owen.

He was wearing nothing but a pair of expensive looking swim trunks and even more expensive-looking sunglasses. I couldn't help giving his body a once-over, realizing that he must have women do this all the time. He grinned as if he knew exactly what I was doing, and instead of feeling embarrassed, I was glad I had looked.

I had felt how strong he was every time he had touched me in the past couple days, but I hadn't expected those muscles to be so... uncovered. There wasn't a hair on his body below his ears. Indeed, even his face was completely clean shaven, and his square jaw accentuated the obvious hardness of his muscles.

I knew I was beginning to stare when he said, "What are you up to?"

I opened my mouth but no words came out. I pointed behind me at the general vicinity of the woman in the sky, my head not allowing itself to turn away from the Greek god who stood before me.

He smiled. "I haven't been parasailing in a while, but I still have a 'chute at my place. Would you like to go with me?"

Once again, he was trying to get me to go to his

house. I smiled, this time managed to stutter a response. "I can't, I-"

He cut me off, removing his sunglasses. His blue eyes squinted immediately, but it had the desired effect as he stared at me and I felt my knees turn to jelly. "Kaylee, no more excuses. I want you to go parasailing with me, and then I want to hear all about being a physician's assistant."

I didn't know how I had managed to resist him this long, but I lost the battle with my own common sense at that moment. As soon as I decided to go with him, I regained most of my confidence. "Sounds great! I just have to drop my book off at my room, and we can go."

He gestured to me to lead the way. As I walked past him, he put his hand on my back, guiding me as I headed to the row of rooms Jack had rented out. Normally I would have shrugged him off, but his touch felt so good...

CHAPTER FIVE

The walk to his beach house was pretty quick, and he spent the time talking to me about my job. I kept the details as sparse as possible, not wanting him to think that I was too interested. However, with every look he gave me, I found my resistance breaking down. He walked beside me, occasionally bumping into me a little bit, and I wondered if I would even make it to his place before my defenses broke down completely.

As we neared his house, I gasped. Oh sure, he never told me it was his until we got close, but I could see it from about a mile away. It was huge, with gigantic bay windows looking out over the ocean. There were balconies off of every bedroom. It looked more like another resort than somebody's home. *Why not?* I asked myself. *With all the money in the world, I might do the same thing.*

I had wanted to check it out, but I never got the chance. Naturally, he had somehow sent a message to the dock that we were going parasailing without me even noticing. A parachute with two harnesses was already set up and ready for us to go on the dock attached to his mansion.

"Are we ready to go?" Owen asked as we approached the dock.

The owner of the speed boat looked like an experienced sea hand, typing on his tablet quickly. "I'm all set, Mr. Parker, and the weather is good for the next few hours." Owen nodded, and we began to get into the harnesses.

The captain strapped us into what looked like a big swing for two. I began to get nervous as he explained what we should do in an emergency, but nodded my head and acted unafraid. There was no way I was going to back out of this now. This was a vacation adventure, and I was going to treat it that way.

Before the boat started moving, Owen reached over and plucked the flower from my hair, raising it to his nose and taking a breath.

"Ah, plumeria. These usually grow in Hawaii, but I see no reason why they wouldn't thrive here," he said softly.

"I wondered what it was. I think it might be my new favorite." I grinned at him as he pocketed the small flower, making sure it was safe as the speedboat's engine revved.

We rode out to the designated area on the back

of the boat. I gripped the straps of the "swing" tightly, getting more and more nervous by the moment. Another man kept the tether reeled in while the captain looked back at us. "Are you ready?" he yelled at us.

Owen looked at me. "Are you afraid of heights?" he asked.

I smiled at him. It was probably pretty obvious. "A little," I confessed.

He smiled back. "Me too." He gave a thumbs-up to the captain. The captain hit the throttle as the assistant freed the release on the tether. Suddenly, I felt myself being pulled off the back of the boat. The captain had warned us that this is what it would feel like, but I panicked a little anyway. Soon, however, we were completely clear of the boat and climbing. I felt the parachute bring us higher and higher, and I found myself growing more and more excited. When Owen let out a whoop of joy, I joined in with him, screaming my own lungs out.

The captain had told us that the tether was four-hundred feet long but that we would only be going up about half that distance. Still, as we reached the apex of our flight, I could see for miles around. Owen grabbed at my hand, and I looked over at him and gave him a huge grin.

After about fifteen minutes of looking at all the scenery and feeling the wind blow us around, I could feel the tether reeling us back in. We got closer and closer to the boat, and soon we lifted our legs up, getting ready to land. I could see Owen's eyes on my toned legs, which were probably the sexiest part of my body. *Let him look,* I thought, *I've been checking him out all day.*

Within another few moments, we were safely back on the boat. The assistant helped us out of our harnesses, and I took a seat. Owen pulled a cooler out of a storage compartment, and inside was ice and a bottle of champagne. He had already popped the cork, pulling two glasses out before I had a chance to refuse. The label on the bottle looked fancy.

He poured two servings and set the bottle back down in an ornate bottle holder. He sat next to me, not shy at all about how close the two of us were sitting. He handed me a glass, and I accepted. Our cups clinked softly together as he toasted, "To trying new things on vacation."

I grinned back. "To vacation," I agreed. We both took a sip.

He looked out to the sea, his blue eyes seeming to search the waves for something. "I was lying when I said I was just a little scared of heights. I'm terrified of them," he said.

I looked at him, unsure if he was telling the truth. "We didn't have to go parasailing, you know."

He laughed. "I've gotten used to them," he said. "Not only do I fly everywhere, I spend a lot of time in Dubai, and the tower they put me in is the highest in the world. As long as I don't go too close to the windows, I'm okay."

I sipped the wine again. "Dubai? Where is that?"

"It's part of an oil-rich state in the Middle East," he explained. Then he smiled and looked at me.

"But I'm no Wikipedia page on the subject. What are you afraid of?"

"Me?" I asked. The sudden question threw me off. *I'm afraid of dying alone*, came my immediate thought, but there was no way I could say that. It wasn't even quite true, but the last man I had been with had taken advantage of me, and I was still feeling vulnerable. So I said the next best thing. "I'm afraid there's no decent men left in this world."

Owen smiled. "All the good ones are either taken or gay," he said.

I leaned in a little closer. "So which one are you?" I asked.

"Indecent," he said without a moment's hesitation. I looked down, seeing if he meant what I thought he meant. "Made you look," he said.

I slapped his chest without thinking, the hardness of his muscles once again taking me by surprise. *He must work out every day*, I thought. He knew what I had felt just then, and immediately his eyes were on me, on my body. He looked at me with a hunger in his eyes.

"So," I said, trying to break him out of it. "I should probably get back to the resort. My family probably thinks I wandered off into the ocean by now."

"That's already been taken care of. Jack has let your family know that you wandered off with me," he said.

I blushed and looked down at my feet. They knew my reputation all too well and were probably already making assumptions. "Great," I said. "We might as well take our time then."

"My thinking exactly," he said. "I saw you looking at my house earlier. Would you like a tour?"

I hesitated. The place had been huge, and I had wanted to check it out, but now I wavered. My inner voice popped up again. Go! Check out the billionaire's mansion! You*'re on vacation, and besides, when are you going to get another chance like this?*

My inner voice was right. It was a vacation. I wasn't about to fall in love like I always seemed to do, and even if I did, my vacation was going to be over tomorrow anyway.

"I'd love a tour," I said. I could feel my smile beaming, but I still don't think it was as big as his was.

CHAPTER SIX

He opened the huge oak door to his house and ushered me inside. I stood at the entrance for a moment, not wanting to track sand all over, but he just kicked his sandals off near the wall and walked right in. I followed suit.

I knew that Jack had been staying here when he met Emma, and that he had stopped sleeping here to stay in her cabana house by the beach. I'm sure if Emma had known what he was giving up to be with her, she would have insisted on living here instead.

Owen took me on the grand tour, showing me the kitchen, the living room, the dining room, and the backyard where he hosted parties. A beautiful gazebo stood in one corner, and I thought about how much I'd like to have a gazebo like that in my backyard someday.

An open door revealed some stairs leading downward. "What's down there?" I asked.

He shrugged. "Nothing really. Just where I hang out when it's just me and close friends."

I waited. "Well, can I see it?"

He looked at me quizzically. "You want to see my Man Cave?"

I laughed. "Of course I want to see your Man Cave."

I walked down the wooden stairs. The light from the basement stairwell only reached slightly into the room, so I had to squint in order to see. Owen switched a switch and the room lit up.

A tattered, comfortable looking, leather couch sat in front of a big screen TV. One of every video game system made since the Super Nintendo was hooked up, with controllers and games neatly filed in drawers on either side of the entertainment center. An old pinball machine whirred to life in the corner. Neon signs flickered on over a wooden bar with every kind of liquor I could think of.

"What do you think?" he asked.

"It's... a Man Cave, alright," I said.

He walked behind the bar, immediately picking up a washcloth and a glass. "What can I get you, young lady?" he inquired.

"Were you a bartender in a past life?" I quipped, taking a seat on one of the stools. "I'll take a Malibu on the rocks."

"A good vacation choice," he said. "I play bartender every chance I get. Someday, when I retire, I'm going to open up a bar."

"Bars are too much trouble," I said. "You have to get a liquor license, jump through all sorts of hoops, and then you have to make the place chic."

"Too true. Would you like a splash of pineapple juice?" he asked, pouring a drink for himself as well.

"That sounds delicious." He set the drink down in front of me and I took a sip. "When I retire, I want to open a bed and breakfast. Just a few rooms, I'll cook up eggs and pancakes every morning, my husband can gossip with the guests..."

"So this is a group thing, huh? You're going to drag your future husband into this scheme of yours as well?" he asked, a teasing tone to his voice.

I shrugged and took another drink. "It's my fantasy, so yes, he's into the scheme."

"What other fantasies do you have?" he wondered, leaning in.

Danger! Danger, Kaylee! I thought. The comment was clearly sexual in nature, and if I spent all day talking about my fantasies, he'd have me right where he wanted me...

I tossed the rest of the drink back. "Pour me another, barkeep, and don't skimp on the pineapple juice," I said. Another drink was poured for me, quick as could be. I reached into my pocket and opened up my wallet, fishing out a dollar bill. I slid it across the table toward him. "Don't spend it all in one place."

He grabbed the pocket of his shirt and opened it towards me, leaning in. I picked the dollar back up and tucked it in the open space. As I stuffed the bill in, I felt his muscular chest again, but I didn't pull my hand away.

"What kind of fantasies can a man like you have, anyway? What can a billion of these not buy?" I asked, moving the dollar bill against his chest more.

His eyes flickered, a flash of sadness behind them for just a moment. "I'm still a human being, you know. One with wants and needs. Do you really want to know what I want the most?"

I leaned in closer. "Tell me."

He pulled away. *Was it something I said?* I thought. I didn't know what I had done to offend him, to make him pull back, but then he walked around the bar, and sat down at the stool next to me. His voice got even lower as he leaned in conspiratorially.

"Jack and I were supposed to hang out last year at his vacation. Even though he brought his secretary, it was supposed to be kind of a bachelor party that we'd never have, because we both knew that we'd never find someone who could look past all this," he said as he waved his hand in the air, as if this Man Cave were the measure of his wealth.

"But, after I didn't see him the entire trip, we shared a flight back to New York. He had met someone, and he wouldn't shut up about her." His voice got lower, as if he were ashamed. "How witty she was. How fantastic in bed she was. When I found out that she hadn't even known about his money, you can't even imagine how jealous I was. When I met Emma, I was immediately attracted to her." The tone of his voice betrayed the fact that it was more than just an attraction.

It was a startling confession. The suave billionaire must have known that the way to a woman's heart was not to basically confess their unrequited love for their younger sister, but he had done just that.

"But Jack had never been happier, so I kept my distance. Oh, we spoke, and of course I flirted with her, but it was painful. She has no idea of course." He looked at me, and his eyes conveyed an unspoken *And I'd like to keep it that way.*

I nodded, unwilling to interrupt him. "But, I found out that Emma had a big sister. One who was somehow even more beautiful and just as witty. One who was having just as much problem finding happiness as her little sister had. One who I was finally going to meet at a wedding."

He sighed, taking the dollar bill out of his shirt pocket and throwing it on the floor, looking at it with disgust. "If I could have one thing, one fantasy, it would be a time machine, so I could go back in time before you had me pegged as an asshole billionaire. I'd let you fall for me like I've already fallen for you."

I'm his fantasy, I realized. I was speechless, but there was no need to let words do the talking. In the back of my mind, the cautious voice in my head was telling me that he might be making all this up just to get in my panties, but that voice was quickly drowned out. I looked into his blue windows of the soul, and knew that he was being completely genuine.

I leaned in and pressed my lips against his. As my tongue darted into his mouth, I could taste the coconut liquor on his lips, and I drank him in. He returned the kiss eagerly, wrapping his hands around my back and bringing me in closer. I pulled him into me, his skin smooth on my fingers. We broke from the kiss and I marveled at his huge pecs and abs, eying him hungrily. I knew he was looking at me the same way, and it turned me on.

My hands found their way to his chest, my nails running up and down his body immediately. He shuddered, obviously in shock that his fantasy was about to come true. My t-shirt was next, and with one deft motion, he untied the back of my bikini top as well. He didn't remove it, but rather allowed it to hang loosely for a moment. I smiled at him, putting my hands over my small breasts for a moment before peeling off the bikini top.

It was at that moment that his lust hit a breaking point. He stood up from the bar stool, lifting me up like I was weightless. I wrapped my legs around him and he held me up. My hair fell into his face, getting in the way of our kisses as our bodies pressed together. I began to grind against him, pushing my body into his even more, as he walked over to the couch. He set me down gently, then kissed the length of my neck, drinking in my body. He kissed each of my breasts for just a few moments, my nipples hardening as soon as they felt his tongue against them. Then he continued moving down.

I felt a momentary pang of panic as he

unbuttoned my jean shorts, but it passed as soon as I looked into his eyes. I saw nothing but honest love emanating from him, and I wanted him to continue. I needed him.

He worked the jean shorts down my long legs before untying my bikini bottoms. Those, too, were off my legs in a heartbeat. He began to kiss up my legs, past my knees, working towards my thighs...

I knew where he was going, and I knew my own body better than he did. After all the walking, the parasailing, and the alcohol, I wasn't at my freshest. I grabbed him by the hair, but he kept moving up. "Owen, you don't have to... to..." I stopped as his tongue met my labia, unable to speak any longer.

The guys I had been with never bothered to give me head, but I could honestly say that that first time Owen performed cunnilingus on me, he changed my world. He devoured me, giving everything that he had to my pleasure. His tongue moved up and down in ways that I hadn't thought possible. As he grabbed my legs and positioned himself to better hit my pleasure center, I knew that I wouldn't be able to last long.

As I had when we were on the back of the boat, getting ready to parasail, I felt myself begin to lose control. I could feel myself floating, being dragged up and off by nature itself. Only this time, I felt more prepared. I didn't panic, I let it happen. I let myself be lifted into the sky by the pleasure that coursed through my body, and as I felt myself climbing, I could feel my muscles become more and more tense.

"Oh, Owen," I moaned as I reached into the heavens. My hands went from Owen's hair to the arm of the couch behind me as I braced myself for my orgasm. I felt his tongue lift me higher and higher, until I felt like I was above the clouds. My muscles began to jerk as I found myself in heaven, the pleasure so intense that I squeezed my legs around Owen's head as the most intense orgasm of my life rocked my body.

As the pleasure subsided a little, I felt myself dip back below the clouds. I relaxed my grip on Owen's head, expecting him to stop, but he just kept going at the same pace and intensity. I felt the wind beneath my sails again as I rose even higher into the clouds. I felt my body begin to sweat as my eyes rolled back into my head and I orgasmed again.

As this second orgasm subsided, I grabbed Owen by the hair and pulled hard. He immediately came up to my mouth and kissed me, as he worked his swimming trunks off. I could feel his erection press up against me and I wanted it more than anything.

"Please, Owen. Please, make love to me," I begged, rocking my body up against his. He moved his lips to my ear, kissing me lightly.

I continued to try to take him inside of me. "Wait," he said, but I couldn't help myself. I needed him, worse than I had needed any man in my life. "Wait!" he insisted, but I didn't listen. I heard him groan into my ear, and he obviously wanted this as much as I did. With what must have been Herculean strength, he managed to break from me. I watched his toned ass as he moved to his entertainment center and opened the drawer labeled "Sega Genesis". He reached his hand in and pulled out a condom.

As he turned, I finally got a look at his manhood. It was long and thick, and incredibly sexy. He tore open the wrapper of the condom and rolled it onto his cock. I was on birth control, but I appreciated the gesture and I wasn't about to stop him. He quickly returned, finding the exact position he had left.

"Now I'm ready," he said, and immediately began to push into me. I was so wet, but I could still feel him expanding me, stretching me. I dug my nails into his back and bit his shoulder as he filled me completely. I heard him moan with pleasure as I enveloped him. He whispered into my ear, "I've wanted this for so long."

He pushed himself up with his huge biceps, making the muscles flex and gleam in the light. I raked my fingernails from where they had dug into his back down his sides, and he began to thrust inside me in earnest. His body, already with a light sheen of moisture on it, began to sweat as he pumped in and out of me. I moved my hands to my breasts as they swayed underneath him, as he growled with appreciation.

No man I had ever been with had the rhythm and strength of Owen Parker. With every mighty thrust within me, I felt like he was going deeper and deeper. I looked at his backside as his hips undulated like a snake and his ass moved back and forth. "Oh, that is so hot," I moaned.

A drop of sweat fell from his forehead right before he pulled out of me, turning me on my side. He got behind me on the couch, putting one arm beneath my neck and the other over my body, grabbing one breast in each hand. I lifted one leg and allowed him to enter my nether regions before wrapping his legs up in mine.

We writhed together as if we were one person. I felt his smooth, hairless chest against my back as he pushed into me with increased intensity. I could feel him squeezing me in tighter, his arms pulling me into him, trying to absorb me. I wanted him to absorb me. With him inside me, I felt whole.

I felt his thrusts get more and more frantic. I knew that he was about to have his own orgasm, and I wanted to be right there with him. My hand moved south, and I began to vigorously rub myself. With him filling me and my own direct stimulation, I felt myself rising towards orgasm even quicker than before.

As my body began to tense up, I felt his breath in my ear. It was coming in ragged bursts now, as he was clearly getting close. "Yes," I moaned. I felt myself rising on the parasail again, only this time I wasn't alone. This time, I had someone in the seat next to me, rising himself, becoming closer to me.

As he slammed into me, groaning into my ear with release, I felt my own body seize up. He hugged me even closer to him as our two bodies moved in tandem, our feet rubbing against each other, our bodies sliding against each other. He continued to breathe in my ear, and with every shudder he made, I got another rush of delight. We flew through the clouds, lifted by a parachute of pleasure, for what seemed like forever.

Finally, he finished. He pulled out of me quickly, before he began to grow soft, and disposed of the condom. He lay back down behind me, snuggling up against me. His big arms wrapped around me, and I felt completely safe and warm. For several minutes, we laid like this while our breathing returned to normal. I should have known better than to ruin the moment, but something had been bothering me.

"What's with the condoms in the Sega Genesis drawer?" I asked.

He burst out laughing, the motion making me shiver with delight. "It's kind of an inside joke. I lost my virginity during a particularly intense game of Sonic the Hedgehog 2. From then on, I made sure that I always had a condom available while I played."

I smiled. What a normal thing to have happen to a billionaire. *I should stop thinking about him like that,* I thought. He was just a man, and I needed to stop thinking of him as some kind of inhuman thing.

"Do you still have it?" I asked.

"What, the condom? No, I tossed it out," he said.

I turned around, my breasts brushing against his chest. "No, silly. Sonic 2. I haven't played in years."

He grinned the biggest smile I had seen since I met him. He pushed himself off the couch and went to the TV, unwrapping two controllers. I admired that ass of his as he set up the game, thinking that this was the kind of vacation I had always wanted.

***

We sat there, already completely comfortable with our naked bodies, and played Sonic 2 for about half an hour. Somehow he cheated, because there was no way he could beat me that many times in a row without cheating. Halfway through a game, I heard his phone begin to ring. He set the ancient controller down on his knees and dug around in his swim trunks for his phone. I kept playing, not bothering to pause it for him. This might be my only chance to win a round.

Someone was talking on the other end as he picked up the controller and kept playing. "Yeah. Yeah. Okay. Yeah. We'll be there." He put the controller down and started to go to the TV.

"Wait! I'm going to beat you this time!" I said when I noticed him reaching for the video game console.

He laughed. "I forfeit. You won all the rounds," he said as he reached for the power button again.

"That's not fair!" I exclaimed. "You're just giving up because you know you're going to lose."

He looked at me for about a half-second, then quickly ran back to the couch and lifted up the controller, picking up where he had left off. It was a close one, but I eked out a victory by a smaller margin than I should have. My victory dance was probably a little excessive, but he didn't seem to mind watching me prance around his Man Cave.

"When you're done looking silly, we have a party to go to. We'll have to hurry to make it on time," he said.

"Party?" I asked. "I didn't hear about a party."

"Robbie just set it up. He wants everyone on his yacht for a cocktail party tonight. I know he's wanted to get everyone on that boat for a while now," he said.

I bit my lip. It was a habit I had passed on to Emma, though she did it more than I did. "Owen, I only had a four-day weekend here. I leave tomorrow afternoon. I was hoping we could spend the rest of the evening together," I said.

He looked at me like I was concerned about nothing. "We'll have the rest of the evening, during and after the party." I continued to look at him, thinking about how just a few minutes ago he was telling me how much he had wanted me, and now he wanted to go to a party. However, his features softened. "You're right. I'll call him back and tell him we aren't coming."

"No!" I blurted out. "No, you're right, let's go to the party. Can you get a ride for me back to the hotel? I have to get dressed."

He hesitated for a moment, then said, "Of course. I'll get ready here and we can meet at the boat." He threw his swim trunks on and then watched me get my own jeans and t-shirt on. I carried my bathing suit with me as he called his driver to come pick me up. He waited on the front porch (which was as beautiful as the back porch) with me while the car came.

"I'll see you there, sweetheart," he said. Sweetheart. *The name fit me well,* I thought. He kissed me on the cheek, then disappeared back in the house.

⚜

CHAPTER SEVEN

As I entered my hotel room, the word still rang in my head. *Sweetheart*. Did that mean we were a couple now? Was this just a way to keep him in my good graces for the rest of the time I was here at the resort? I was so confused.

I had only brought three dresses on this vacation. One was my bridesmaid dress, and I couldn't wear that. I had a slutty red dress that I could use to really impress him, or...

I picked up my favorite dress in the world. It looked like it was out of the 1950s, like it could be in some Marilyn Monroe film. It was light pink with warm brown dots all over it. It had a pretty belt that went around the waist, and it flared out at the bottom. I put it on, the fabric soft and light, perfect for a tropical evening.

I carefully did my makeup, going with a light, natural look. I didn't bother doing anything special with my hair, instead just tying the long dark locks up in a simple ponytail. We were going to be out on a boat, and I had seen enough TV to know there would be wind.

It didn't take me long to walk down to the resort dock, where Robbie's yacht bobbed happily in the water. I grinned with excitement as I saw it. Tall masts rose with graceful ropes attached like strange streamers proclaimed it a sailing vessel rather than something with a motor. It reminded me of an old-fashioned pirate ship, and knowing Robbie, I wouldn't have been surprised to see a pirate flag waving from the top mast.

Emma waved as she saw me approach, Jack at her side and looking like he was enjoying his honeymoon. I knew Robbie would already be on the boat, but I didn't see Owen yet. The thought that I beat him getting ready made me giggle. I had to remember to call him a girl later for taking so long to get pretty.

I stepped onto the deck, carefully picking my way to where Emma sat sipping on champagne. Jack grinned and handed me a glass of the bubbly liquid.

"Where's yours?" I asked, noticing he didn't have a drink. Jack grinned and pointed his head towards what I assumed was where the steering wheel would be.

"Robbie has a strict 'no alcohol for anyone sailing' policy. Since I'm helping man the sails, nothing but water for me."

I nodded and glanced around the beautiful yacht. It was smaller than I expected a billionaire's yacht to be, but it was incredibly beautiful. Wooden decks gleamed, and from what I could see of the interior, it was furnished as nicely as Owen's house.

"How do you race on this?" I asked Jack, pointing towards a series of deck chairs facing out at the ocean. I couldn't imagine that would be very helpful in a racing situation.

Robbie laughed coming around the corner, his green eyes bright. "This isn't my racing yacht. This is my Caribbean yachting yacht. I like to race in solo competitions, and this one is just too big to handle by myself."

My lips made an "O" shape, as I nodded and glanced around. I knew nothing about sailing, but with as many sails as I could see, it was easy to understand this ship would need a crew, especially in harsh weather.

"Solo competitions? Isn't that dangerous?" I asked.

Robbie shrugged. "It can be. I just don't trust anyone else on the water but me. You should come watch me race sometime. I think you'd enjoy it." Robbie grinned, launching into a description of what the races were like. His eyes shone with excitement at talking about the sport he loved. He was a different person out here on the water. On land he was the ever drunk, screw-up younger brother with nothing to do. Out here, he was the captain of his world, and he took it seriously.

I was about to ask him more, but Jack called out a greeting to Owen, and I turned.

"Hey, Owen! Glad you decided to join us. I got worried when Kaylee arrived by herself. I was sure the two of you would be arriving together," Emma called, slurring her speech a little. Jack kept a straight face, but I was sure I saw Emma wink. I sighed. I was never going to live this down.

"Who's to say we didn't? Maybe we did and we're just trying to confuse you?" Owen gave me a wink of his own as he sauntered across the deck. I couldn't help but blush, turning out towards the ocean so my sister wouldn't see.

"Sure. The girl who falls in love at the drop of a hat and the man who can't help but charm every female he runs across, both of whom disappeared *together* for an entire afternoon *together*, arrived separately in order to confuse us. Sounds perfectly legit," Emma said. I wondered just how many glasses of champagne she'd had in order to spout these blunt truths so freely.

A silence fell across the deck as everyone avoided eye contact. Jack frowned at her and snatched her glass. "I think that's good for now, Emma. Why don't you go sit down and look for dolphins?"

She pouted for a moment, looking at her glass, but then trotted off to a deck chair. She swayed as she walked and it wasn't because the boat was moving. Jack just shook his head at her and hid her champagne.

Robbie broke the awkward silence, announcing

that everyone was aboard and we were shoving off. I glanced up at the sails, expecting them to unfurl and propel us across the blue water, but instead a motor revved and we started moving.

"Don't worry, we'll use the sails. We just need to get out in open water," Robbie assured me when he saw my disappointed look. It was only a few minutes before Robbie deemed the wind right and turned off the motor. Robbie, Jack, and an experienced looking crewman worked the sails, the boat suddenly flying across the water.

I stood at the bow, the warm wind skimming the ocean's surface. The water was turning from tropical aqua to a sapphire blue as we headed away from land. It wasn't long before all I could see was the gently rippling horizon in every direction.

Owen leaned against the railing beside me, close enough to touch if we wanted, but far enough away that the others wouldn't tease. "You look like you've seen a miracle," he said.

"I've never been out on the ocean before. Heck, I'd never even seen the ocean before I got here. It's spectacular." I gazed out at the water as it started to catch the light from the setting sun. The waves shone with tiny mirrors as the water began to turn golden with the sunset.

"You're doing well for a first-timer. Have you been on a boat before?"

I shook my head. "The only 'boat' I've been on is a paddle-boat at Gray's Lake. But even though I loved that, this is so much better."

Owen stared out at the horizon, nodding gently.

He was about to speak when we hit a wave and the boat lurched. I wasn't expecting it, but Owen caught my hand and steadied me.

"No falling overboard. I don't really like swimming in my nice clothes," he said with an easy grin. He held onto my hand, not letting it go despite the fact that I no longer needed it. I was glad; I didn't want him to.

We stood there, looking out at the water as the sun kissed the horizon and turned the world to gold and crimson. It was spectacular, but over in an instant, as the dark night surrounded our tiny boat. It was so beautiful I was sure it had to be a dream. The sky began to twinkle, the sky full of more stars than I had ever seen. With Owen's hand in mine, I was sure I would wake up at any moment. It was all just too good to be true.

Owen slipped his arm around my shoulders, his warmth seeping into me as the heat from the sun dissipated. I knew that Emma, Jack and Robbie could clearly see us, but I didn't care. Despite my best intentions, I was falling hard for this charming man. I glanced over at him, taking in his golden hair, perfect cheekbones and broad shoulders, wondering what I had done to deserve this moment.

The boat dipped again, and Owen pulled me more tightly to him. I could smell his cologne mixing with the salt in the air. He turned, his eyes as deep as the water, and kissed me .

For a moment, I let myself forget everything but that kiss. There was no island, no flight tomorrow, no having to return home alone, just this moment wrapped up in his embrace. I knew this would never happen again, that I would never get another moment like this. Tomorrow I would go back to my life in Iowa, he would go back to his life in Dubai, and that would be the end. Our worlds were just too different for it to happen any other way.

"Hey! No making out on my boat!" Robbie yelled at us. I felt the blush flare across my cheeks as Owen let me go. I looked back to see Jack giving a small golf clap, but at least Emma was passed out on the deck chair.

I looked over at Owen and he gave me a grin. They were going to tease us both until the end of time, but, at that moment, I didn't care. It was worth it.

"You two lovebirds ready to head back?" Jack asked. I looked down at my watch surprised that we had been out on the water for over two hours at that point. Emma was snoring softly on the deck chair. I looked out at the water and could see the lights of the resort coming back into view.

Owen turned to me. "You want to finish that tour of my place?" He somehow managed to keep all the innuendo out of his voice. I glanced at Jack and Robbie as they trimmed the sails. Emma would be waking up soon.

"It would mean they would see us leaving together," I said softly. Owen kissed my cheek.

"I don't care if you don't," he whispered back. I grinned and grabbed his hand, ready to go explore his mansion. I was on vacation, and I was going to have a good time.

***

"You sure you don't want me to come to the airport with you?" Owen asked as he lounged on my bed. He had his head in his hand, elbow bent as he watched me finish packing my bags. I thought about jumping him again right there. We had just come from his beach house so I could pack after a fantastic night together. I was going to be sore for days as it was, so I decided against it.

"No, I'd rather go by myself." No need for him to see me freak out getting on the plane. I would rather he not remember me as a terrified mess. "Thank you though."

He gave me a radiant smile. "You sure you have to leave? I can have my private jet fly you home."

I thought about it for a long moment. It was such a tempting offer. "I can't. I have to work tomorrow."

He made a face that told me he clearly wasn't impressed by my excuse. I laughed and crawled up on the bed next to him. "I had to fight to get this much time off. Besides, I like my job."

"I thought you said you wanted to open a B&B?"

I gave him an impressed look. He had been paying attention.

"I do, but there's no way I can afford to right now. I've got student loans out the wazoo, and I don't feel right having Emma pay them off."

Owen nodded. I knew we were both avoiding the subject we really wanted to talk about. What would happen after this vacation? There was no fake marriage ceremony tying us together, no paparazzi that would be hounding me everywhere I went. He had no reason to visit me, and despite his heartfelt words, I just couldn't see us continuing a real relationship.

A knock on the door announced my driver to the airport. I looked at Owen and slowly stood up from the bed to answer the door. The driver took my bags, wheeling them to the waiting car while giving me some privacy to say goodbye.

"Owen," I started, but I couldn't find the words to make this hurt less. Goodbyes were always hard for me.

Owen didn't say a word, he just wrapped me up in his arms and kissed me.

I've never wanted a kiss to last forever as much as I did then.

When we finally broke apart, I turned and ran, unable to look him in the eye. I wanted that moment to be perfect in my mind forever. If I didn't actually say goodbye, then maybe it wouldn't actually happen.

Owen stood out on the porch of my room, his blonde hair blowing softly in the wind as the car rolled away. He held up one hand in a wave, growing smaller until I could no longer see him. I cried all the way to the airport.

CHAPTER EIGHT

"Kaylee, you have a new patient in Room Four and the man in Room Five is puking again." Allie, one of the ER unit assistants, sidled up to me, handing me the freshly made chart for the patient in Room 4. "I have Mr. Smith in Room Three ready for his EKG, and we are just waiting on Dr. Gregory to come consult. By the way, how was your sister's wedding?"

"It was great. I think Iowa needs an ocean," I said with a grin. Allie giggled in agreement as I flipped open the battered blue plastic binder and started scanning through the patient's history. *Thomas Birch. Male, age sixteen, fell skateboarding. Complains of 8/10 pain in wrist. No known allergies or other pertinent medical history.* It was looking like a fairly routine-but-busy day.

At least the busy day would keep my mind off a certain someone. "We'll probably need X-rays," I said after reading the file. "Will you find out what the wait time down in Radiology is? And go ahead and let Marta know that Mr. Birch can have the standard pain med protocol. For the man in Room Five, make sure he has a bucket. I'll check on him next and see if we can't up the medication in his IV."

Allie nodded and hurried off to find the nurse. I tucked the chart under my arm and headed to the room. A young man stared up at me with big eyes, trying to be brave as his eyes betrayed the fear crawling up inside of him. I knew he was taking in my white lab coat, the chart under my arm, and the dark blue scrubs, hoping that I would be able to make things better.

"Are you the doctor?" he asked. His mom looked up, her face anxious.

"I'm Kaylee, and I'm a physician's assistant. I'd like to take a look at your arm, if that's okay with you."

He nodded slowly as I washed my hands and sat down on a wheelie chair by his gurney. He started to tell me how the accident happened, and I listened as I looked him over, asking questions and jotting notes. The poor kid's arm had an extra bend in it and was swollen. It looked really painful. Quickly I scribbled down my observations onto the chart. *Probable closed distal radius fracture: no open wound. X-ray, consult with ortho, cast vs surgery,* my mind ran through the diagnosis, thinking of the next steps.

"You're going to have to lay off the ollies for a little while with this. It looks like you have a distal radius fracture, or a broken wrist. We'll need an X-ray to know for sure exactly what's broken." I gently placed his damaged wrist back in his lap. He looked at me with big eyes. "As long as it is just a simple break, it shouldn't be a problem. In a little bit, someone will be in to take you to Radiology to get your X-rays. Once we get them back, we'll have a better idea of what to do next."

"Is he going to need surgery?" The boy's mother's face was pale and drawn.

"We won't know until after the X-rays. Hopefully not, though," I answered honestly. The mother nodded and pressed her lips into a thin line. "I'll make sure to let you know as soon as we get the films. Can I get you anything?"

The boy and his mother shook their heads, and I thanked both of them, washed my hands and left the room. I could hear a trauma alert going off for Section Three. I was Section Two, but I still mentally prepared myself. If it was a rough one, I would have to hop over and help.

"Kaylee, you have a phone call, line two," Allie called out to me from the desk. I went into the nurse's station and found a chair, opening the chart to write my notes and orders before picking up the phone.

"ER, this is Kaylee, how may I help you?"

"If I wanted to see you again, would I have to be a patient?" The voice caught me off guard for a moment. No way it was Owen. As much as I wanted it to be him, there was no way a suave, handsome billionaire was going to call me at the ER.

"Owen?" I hoped I didn't sound as squeaky through the phone as I did to my own ears.

"Are you in the habit of seeing many people?" I could hear his handsome smile through the phone. Out in the parking lot an ambulance siren sounded its arrival. I glanced up, checking the status boards, seeing two more patients pop up for my area. Hopefully the trauma wouldn't need my help because this day was starting to look a little hectic.

"If you came into this ER without a major trauma, I would give you one. It is too busy today and we are just getting busier." I scribbled out my signature on the bottom of the order page and handed the chart to the charge nurse for order input.

"Alright then. What time do you get off work?"

"7:30. Though it's usually a little later just to finish paperwork. Why?" Three new patients in the waiting room.

"I'll give you a call then." There was a smile in his voice as the line shifted to silence. I placed the receiver back on the phone, a small smile forming on my lips. It was something to look forward to at the end of my shift. The medics wheeled an elderly woman with what appeared to be a broken hip into the trauma room. At least they weren't going to need the backup, I thought to myself as I headed to room five.

My mind kept replaying Owen's voice, the

promise lingering in my head. *I'll give you a call then.* I wondered where he got the ER's phone number, but I realized it wouldn't be that hard to figure out. He knew I worked in an ER and there aren't very many ERs in Des Moines. Heck, it wouldn't be that hard to figure out my private cell number for a man as wealthy as Owen.

I couldn't wait to hear from him again. I stepped into Room Five, my shoes slipping on the floor. Just because we had given him a bucket didn't mean he was using it. I sighed. 7:30 couldn't come fast enough.

෨෬ල ௫௳෬

CHAPTER NINE

My feet hurt so much I was tempted to crawl through the parking lot to get to my car. It was almost 8:00, but the ER had been so packed I hadn't been able to escape any earlier. My boss was not going to be pleased with all the overtime. *Maybe she'll stop pestering me to take extra shifts,* I thought. *Nah, not gonna happen in this lifetime.* The phones had been ringing off the hook, but the desk secretary promised none of the calls had been for me. I had been able to stave off disappointment until I got to my locker and saw I had no messages on my phone.

So much for Owen's call.

As I stepped out of the main ER doors, the frosty night air stung my face. It smelled like it might snow later. I adjusted my scarf to keep the draft out of my coat and began the long walk to my car. I was just hoping it would start with the bitter cold and a semi-dead battery. *Note to self, I really needed to get that fixed.* Just as I reached the curb, my phone began to buzz.

A grin cracked my face as I didn't even pause to look at the caller ID and just hit "Answer".

"Owen?" I asked excitedly into the phone.

A siren from the ambulance room sounded, covering up any response I might of heard. I shot an irritated glare towards the ambulance driver, hoping that Owen was still on the line. I nearly dropped my phone when I looked over though.

Instead of seeing a bashful EMT, there was Owen, leaning against the hood of the ambulance with a bouquet of flowers. He grinned and pushed himself off the red hood and gracefully sauntered over to where I stood, my jaw resting on the pavement. He reached over and gently hit the "End Call" button once he reached me, the contact bringing me out of my shock at seeing him.

"What are you doing here?" My mind was spinning. This had to be a trick my brain was playing. Owen was supposed to be in New York working for Jack, not bringing me flowers at an ER in Des Moines.

"It's a little after 7:30, and I said I would call you. So, I'm calling you," he said quietly. His breath frosted the night air as he spoke and he was close enough that I could almost feel his warmth. I was torn between reaching out and touching him to make sure he was real, or just holding still and letting the dream continue. "These are for you."

He held out the flowers, the plastic lining rustling as he uncovered the protective shell so I could see them. They were soft pink plumeria flowers. I took a deep breath, the sweet fragrance instantly bringing me back to the warm sun and sand. I realized they were the same type of flowers that I had been wearing in my hair.

"They're beautiful," I whispered. My eyes flickered up to look at him and his blue eyes made my heart skip a beat. Even in the garish light of the garage he was gorgeous. I kept hoping he would lean down and kiss me.

"Not as beautiful as you," he whispered, and for a moment, I believed him. He tipped his chin down, angling to bring his mouth to mine, but then a cold wind whipped my hair, flinging the tiny strands that had escaped my messy pony tail into my eyes. It must have hit him too, and I remembered we were standing in the middle of an ambulance receiving bay.

"Thank you," I said as I shivered. Owen looked perfectly warm in his long black wool overcoat, but my own coat was just a little short in the sleeves and let in bursts of cold air whenever I moved. Owen rubbed his gloved hands up and down my arms as soon as he saw I was trembling.

"Let's get you out of the cold. Follow me. I have Chinese food in the car." He reached for my hand and began pulling me gently towards Visitor Parking. I followed eagerly, my stomach growling for something other than hospital coffee and the bagel I stole from the doctor's lounge for lunch.

"Chinese? How did you know to bring exactly what I was craving?" Sesame chicken sounded like the most delicious thing I could imagine at that moment. Well, at least as far as food went...

"I'm just that good..." He smirked like it was true, but it quickly crumbled into a guilty grin when I raised my eyebrows. "Emma told me it was your favorite. I was going to get us reservations at a French restaurant, but she made sure I knew that you could be a grouch at the end of your shifts and I would be risking my life taking you anywhere nice in scrubs. So, I have comfort food and a bottle of wine in the car."

I shook my head. "As much as I hate to admit it, she's right. I probably would have killed you in a horrible and gruesome fashion if I was expected to go out tonight. Chinese gets you extra brownie points."

Owen laughed. My night was infinitely better now, the stresses of the busy shift drifting away on the the last of the winter winds. This was the best way to end a shift. A large black limousine loomed up out of the darkness, purring softly in a corner of the visitors' lot. Owen opened the door and I slid in, the smell of delicious food steaming the tinted windows.

"Oh my god, it smells amazing in here! What all did you get?" I wriggled out of my jacket and bent over one of the brown paper bags, tearing into it like a rabid badger.

"Sesame chicken, lemon chicken, shrimp lomain, spicy beef stir-fry, wontons, dumplings, egg-rolls, and egg fried rice. I hope I got something you like."

I paused long enough in my frantic opening of the bag to grin up at him as he shrugged gracefully out of his coat. "Something I like? You got *everything* I like!"

He relaxed into the seat, rolling his shirt cuffs up, his blue eyes watching me with a twinkle. "Good. I'd hate for you to starve."

I popped a dumpling into my mouth and made a funny face at him, enjoying the way his face crinkled when he laughed. He leaned over and dug into one of the bags until he pulled out a box of fried rice and a pair of chopsticks. He easily started eating the rice with the cheap wooden sticks.

"How'd you learn to do that?" I asked, my mouth full of chicken and dumpling.

"I travel a lot. Japan is a big market and there are a lot of business meetings over dinner." He easily maneuvered the tiny grains of rice into his mouth like it was easy to get them to stick together and not fall all over the leather seats.

"Japan? That must be exciting," I said, taking another bite of sesame chicken. Owen nodded and continued eating his rice.

"I don't get to go there often. I mostly travel to the Middle East and recently to growing parts of Asia and Africa."

"Aren't those parts of the world dangerous?"

"A little. But, it's my job, so I do it. If I go to Japan sometime soon, would you like to go with me?" He lifted his chopsticks neatly to his mouth without a single grain of rice falling off.

"I don't know. Emma's wedding was the first time I've ever left the country. I'm not really big on traveling." I avoided his eyes and dug around in the bag for the egg-rolls.

"What? I thought everyone liked to travel." I could feel the question dancing in his blue eyes as he looked at me. His smile made my heart race. I swallowed my food down hard.

I didn't want to tell him how traveling made me nervous. How I didn't do well away from home or that I loathed the idea of getting on an airplane. The trip for Emma's wedding had taken four shots of whiskey just to get me okay with the idea of the plane taking off. Coming home hadn't been much better.

"I guess I just like home. I like having my life in one place and knowing where everything is. I like road trips to see old friends, but all my favorite things are right here. Why would I want to leave?" I said, a wry smile on my face to disguise the nervousness I felt at even talking about it.

Owen nodded thoughtfully before shrugging and giving me one of his trademarked smiles. "The invitation still stands. I would love to take you to Japan."

"How about you just come with me back to my place?" I held my breath for a moment. I wasn't the one who was usually so bold, but the man did fly out and bring me flowers in a limo.

Owen's face darkened and he set the now empty

box of rice down carefully on the seat.

"I can't, Kaylee. I want to, I really, really want to, but I can't. I have a meeting in the morning."

"Oh," I said. I shrugged. "You sure?" I felt a small twinge of rejection, but I knew he didn't mean it that way. I still felt it, though.

"Kaylee, I wish more than anything I could stay with you tonight, but my flight leaves in an hour and I have to be on it. I'll probably be late for my meeting as is." Owen's blue eyes held mine and I could see the wish reflected in their depths.

"What do you mean, you'll be late as is? It can't be any later than nine and New York is, what, a three hour flight?" I asked slowly.

"The meeting isn't in New York. It's in Abu Dhabi. And I guess technically the meeting isn't tomorrow, but the time changes just get confusing." He looked up apologetically. "I really just wanted to see you again."

"You flew three hours in the wrong direction, just to bring me Chinese food and flowers?"

"Basically."

I was floored. No one had ever done anything like that for me. I felt a warm glow start in my chest, a happiness that made me smile involuntarily. He really did like me.

I leaned over and kissed him. The world was tipsy and wonderful, but somehow incredibly right as our lips met. His hand grabbed the back of my neck, his fingers tangling in the mess of my ponytail, pulling me closer to him. I slid across the leather seat, heat and desire searing through me. All

I wanted was to kiss him, to touch him, to be with him.

His shoulders were strong under my hands, his arms wrapping around me and pulling me into him. I loved the way he smelled, the way he tasted, the way he groaned into my kiss like it was the only thing in the world he had ever wanted. He nibbled on my bottom lip, his tongue dancing with mine as his hands roamed my back and sides.

I began unbuttoning his dress shirt, trying very hard not to simply just rip the buttons off instead. "Kaylee, my flight..." he groaned, but he didn't bother to finish the sentence, letting me continue working on his buttons. The last two, I ripped off.

As soon as his shirt was undone, he reached for my scrub top, lifting it easily over my head and tossing it next to the car door. I giggled as he ran a finger across the strap of the tank top I wore underneath, loving the way his fingers tickled across my skin. He slipped a strap off one shoulder, pushing the bra strap with it, and leaned forward to gently kiss the bare skin. I shivered with anticipation and he pushed the second set of straps off as well.

He licked his lips, his pupils going wide as he traced my collar bone from the shoulder to the center of my breast bone and down into my cleavage. With gentle fingers, he caressed the swells of my breasts peeking out from the tank top. I leaned my head back and let out a sigh of pleasure. This was exactly what I needed after a shift from hell.

"Excuse me sir, but it is time to go to the airport. If you give me the young lady's keys, I will start her car before we leave," the limo chauffeur's voice came over the intercom. I stiffened for a moment, thinking he was watching us, but the privacy screen was still in place.

"If you give him your keys, he'll give us a few more minutes," Owen whispered, brushing a stray strand of dark hair off my cheek. I quickly scrambled for my coat, digging into the pockets for the worn keys. Owen hit the button on the privacy screen, lowering it just enough to let me slide the keys through.

"It's a gray Dodge Neon, third row from the end in the main employee lot," I told the driver before Owen raised the screen back up. I heard the car door open and close, soft footsteps disappearing into the night.

"We have only a couple of minutes," Owen whispered. His eyes were dark with want as he looked me up and down, seeing something that he wanted very badly. "But I just can't say no."

"Then we better make it quick," I replied, kissing him fiercely. I still wasn't looking for a relationship, but when a perfectly muscled man flies three hours to bring you dinner and flowers, it's hard to say no. Especially when your body is screaming yes.

"I don't have a condom," he said softly. I gave him a wicked grin.

"It's okay. I'm on birth control... and I trust you."

He pulled down sharply on my shirt, dragging my bra along with it and exposing my breasts to him. His tongue was on my nipple in an instant, turning it into a hard nub of pleasure in his mouth. I moaned softly, pushing my chest further into his face and reaching to fumble with his belt.

I felt his strong hands slide over mine, easily undoing the button and zipper. I let my hand slide into the opening of his pants, and gasped as I felt his full length ready for my touch. He bit down softly, sending a gentle shock through me and deep into my core. I ran my hands up and down the length of his shaft, feeling him somehow continue to swell.

I pulled at the strings holding my scrub pants to my hips, feeling the comfortable fabric loosen and fall. Owen sped it along, pulling them off as I kicked my clogs off and squirmed out of my pants. As soon as my legs were free, I straddled Owen's lap, kissing him and drawing his tongue into my mouth. His manhood pressed up against my underwear, begging for entrance, and I pushed my hips down into him.

He wrapped one arm around me, his fingers splaying on my back while the other slid my panties to the side. For a glorious moment he sat poised at my entrance, our eyes locked, breathing heavy. Then slowly, so slowly, he slid into me, inch by glorious inch, until I could hold no more.

A shiver of pleasure ran down my spine, and I began rocking back and forth, taking as much of him into me as I could. I never wanted this to end, but I heard the driver open the door and start the engine. Owen pulled me closer to him, thrusting his hips upward with a need that couldn't be stopped.

His hands pulled my hips and back into him, our bodies pressed together, skin rubbing against skin.

The limo slowed to a stop, and I knew we didn't have much time.

"Sir, your flight is in less than twenty minutes," the disembodied voice came through the intercom. Owen's mouth opened as he panted for breath, his body beginning to shake with exertion. I kissed his ear, feeling the velvety softness across my lips as I whispered his name. I wanted him so badly, my entire spine was on fire with longing.

We locked eyes, and his mouth dropped open. I nodded silently, quickly, letting him know it was okay. With a groan of release, Owen spasmed underneath me. I leaned my head against him, his shoulders heaving with effort. He wrapped his arms around me, keeping me close for a moment longer, absorbing me into him.

"That wasn't quite what I expected when I came out here," he murmured into my ponytail as it ran down my back. "I really did just come to bring you flowers."

I giggled and sat up, looking into his perfect face. His hair was mussed and his cheeks flushed, but his eyes held mine like a magnet. I didn't want to ever look away.

"Just don't go telling anyone that all it takes is flowers," I said, only half joking. Owen stretched his neck and kissed the tip of my nose.

"Never."

A knock on the privacy glass broke into our moment as the driver reminded us that we couldn't stay like this forever. Owen kissed me once again before helping me slide onto the seat and back into my pants. We were both dressed again in moments, hardly a trace left behind as Owen opened the door to let me out.

It was dark and cold outside, and all I wanted to do was jump back into the limo and back into Owen's arms. One look at him told me that he felt the same way, but he dutifully opened the driver's door to my beaten up little Neon. Emma had offered to buy me a new one, but this one worked just fine, other than an old battery.

I set the bouquet of flowers and the bags of extra Chinese food in the back seat, coming back around for one more kiss. Owen pulled me close, his lips and tongue hot compared to the winter's night. I kissed him like I was drowning and he was air. Like I needed him in order to breathe. I wasn't sure anymore that I didn't.

The chauffeur coughed discreetly after too short a time. Owen cupped my cheek and gave me one last quick kiss that made my lips tingle for more before turning away. I got into the warm driver's seat and watched as he hurried into the limousine. I raised my hand, not wanting to wave goodbye as the door closed and he drove off into the night.

I drove home, unable to decide if I was happy or sad. The two emotions played tug-of-war, pulling me toward glad I had seen him back to gloomy he had left. I barely made it into pajamas before collapsing in bed, drifting into dreams of Owen.

CHAPTER TEN

Six A.M. came far too early the next day. I groaned and rolled out of bed, the wood floor creaking and cold under my feet. I heard the automatic coffee pot sputter, and I trudged into the kitchen, wishing I could just go back to my dreams with Owen.

The flowers were still in the plastic on my kitchen table. At least I had put them in water before collapsing into bed, so they were still beautiful and vibrant. I lowered the cellophane wrapping and took a deep breath. The soft floral notes didn't remind me of the ocean anymore. They reminded me of someone with blonde hair and deep blue eyes. I smiled, enjoying the memory. I wondered what Owen was doing right then.

I snapped myself out of my thoughts, quickly drinking my coffee so that I could get in the shower. I had another twelve-hour shift in front of me, and no matter how much I would rather spend my morning daydreaming, I had work to do.

***

The ER was busy for the first half of the morning. Patients trickled in at a steady rate, keeping me busy as I raced around between the rooms. Despite the work, I was walking on air. I knew I had a silly smile on my face as I went through my routine, but I didn't care. I had seen Owen last night and it had been fantastic. There was nothing that could spoil this day for me.

"Hey, Kaylee, you have a visitor in the waiting room," Allie called from the desk. I frowned slightly. It couldn't be Owen, he was probably in the middle of a desert by now. No one else would need to come visit me at work, or at least they would know to call first.

"Who is it?"

"Security didn't say."

I handed her the chart I had just finished and told her I would be back in a minute. Visitors weren't allowed in the actual ER, so I headed out to the waiting room to see who it was. The heavy metal doors dividing the waiting room from the ER clanked shut behind me and my heart sank. Standing there joking with the security guard was my ex-boyfriend.

"What are you doing here, Michael?" I asked, trying to stay polite. I had told him a hundred times not to bother me at work. I had been the one to break it off with him, but I got the feeling that he wasn't ready to let me go.

"I came to see you, Kay! I thought we could get lunch." I hated when he called me Kay. *You mean, you thought I would buy you lunch.* He smiled at me like he was doing me the favor. I motioned him away from the security guard to a quiet corner so that we could talk privately.

"Michael, I am really busy today. You know that I've asked you not to visit me at work." I was trying very hard not to get angry. This was just so typical of him.

"I just wanted to see you, Kay. Things have been really hard, and I miss you," he said. His big brown eyes begged me to forgive him, to just love him. I had fallen into those eyes too many times, but never again. This relationship was not healthy. I had spent too much time falling for his tricks to make me do things for him while he did nothing in return.

I thought of all the times he had asked me to take care of things, but how he was always busy or too tired to help me when I needed it. All the condescending comments and cruel teasing. The lack of compliments. How he had made me feel like I was never going to be good enough for anyone but him, but he would keep me because he was just that good of a guy. The way he put me down so I would do anything to please him. An anger I didn't even realize was there bubbled up.

"No, you don't miss *me*," I said, my voice rising. "You miss me taking care of you. You miss me feeling sorry for you because your life is so difficult. You miss me doing all the work to fix it. I am worth so much more than what you tell me I am. I'm tired of it. ***I'm tired of not being appreciated!*** The only time you come around is when you want something." I surprised myself by actually saying it out loud. I had thought those words so many times, but I never had the guts to say it before.

Shock registered in Michael's face. I had never yelled at him like this. "Kay, I do appreciate you! I really do! It's just that things are hard right now. I hate being away from you. My car broke and that job fell through and-"

"I don't care, Michael," I said, cutting him off. "I told you we're done. I meant it. I don't want to take care of you and your problems. It is always all about you. When's the last time you helped me out? Because I can't remember. I can't remember the last time you got me flowers or made me dinner or even offered to help do the dishes. I'm tired of taking care of you and getting nothing in return. I'm going back to work now, and I don't want you to visit me again." I hoped he couldn't see that I was shaking in my Crocs. Everything I hated about our relationship had just kind of spilled out.

As he stood there gaping at me, I realized just how much he had neglected me. Owen flew three hours in the wrong direction just to bring me flowers. In just the week since I had met Owen, he had done more nice things for me than Michael had done in the two years we were together. It wasn't about him spending money on me, either. It was about how he treated me. Owen complimented me. Michael teased. Owen put other people first. Michael never thought of anyone but himself. I didn't like myself when I was with Michael, because he was always putting me down. I was so much better than what Michael told me I was. Looking back, I was shocked that I had let the relationship go on as long as I did.

"Kay, I don't understand. You know things are bad for me right now," he said quietly. His shoulders slumped and he looked so dejected and broken that I almost apologized. *No.* I stood up straighter. *I'm better than this. I deserve someone who wants to take care of me.* Someone like Owen. Just because I felt bad for Michael and his situations didn't mean I had to fix them. Lord knew I had tried enough times, and yet he was still having the same exact problems. They weren't problems I could fix.

"Michael, things are *always* bad for you. You've got to fix it yourself this time. I have patients to see.

Goodbye, Michael. Please don't come back. Ever." I turned quickly and headed back towards the ER. I knew if I turned around and saw his face, I might change my mind. He knew exactly how to look at me to make me cave, and I didn't want to see it. I hurried quickly through the ER doors and back into the safety of the nurse's station.

"You okay?" Allie asked as I leaned against one of the walls. "You look a little pale."

"I just told Michael that I'm tired of taking care of him and that I don't want to see him again," I said weakly. I pressed the palms of my hands against my eyes, shocked that I had actually said those things out loud to him. Allie snorted.

"About time."

I dropped my hands and looked at her. She crossed her arms in front of her chest, her blonde ponytail falling over her shoulder. "What do you mean?"

"Kaylee, you are too nice sometimes. Especially to Michael. He's no good for you. Since the two of you broke up, you've been happier than I've seen you in a long time. And now, you said no to those puppy-dog eyes of his? I don't know what they put in the water in the Caribbean, but if it finally made you get rid of Michael for good, I hope you brought home buckets of it."

It wasn't exactly the water, I thought to myself.

"Thanks Allie." I took a deep breath and smiled. She was right. It was like I had taken a weight off my shoulders that I had never even known I was carrying.

"Don't mention it. Now, since your back and in the mood to tell people off, Dr. James is on hold for your patient in Room Three." She winked and headed back out towards one of the blinking call-lights.

I sighed and tried to summon up some more of the

same fire I had a moment ago. Instead, the only thing I could summon up was the image of Owen smiling.

CHAPTER ELEVEN

I rolled over in bed, listening to the hum of the heater. It was too cold to want to wake up. I smiled as I pulled the covers back up over my head. Since it was my day off, I didn't have to get up at all! Winter was giving its last parting shots at spring, and these would be the last few cold days before warmer weather hung around for good. I snuggled deeper into my blankets, replaying my last phone conversation with Owen.

***

"Are you free Friday?" Owen's voice crackled a little over the long distance connection. I knew he couldn't see me through the phone, but I nodded anyway.

"It's my day off. Why? You want to do something?" I hoped I didn't sound too eager.

"I was thinking I would take you out on a real date. Not just Chinese food in the back of a limo." I could hear the smile in his voice as he remembered exactly what we did in the back of that limo.

"I don't know, I kind of liked Chinese food in the back of the limo." I stopped myself as I started twirling my hair between my fingers. I couldn't help the giddy happiness that bubbled up inside of me at the thought of seeing him again.

"Don't plan anything on Friday, then. I'm taking you out. I want to spoil you."

***

The idea that I would see him tonight, that it would be for a real date night, brought a smile to my face. I was planning on taking a hot shower to shave my legs and everything. *Maybe I'll even go shopping for a new dress,* I thought. I stretched out under the pile of blankets on my bed, debating whether I really even wanted to get out of my very comfy bed at all. Maybe Owen could just join me here.

The buzzer to my apartment building decided that staying in bed was not an option. With a groan, I rolled out of my warm bed, fuzzy socks gliding across the wood floors as I went to the intercom by the door.

"Who is it?" I was expecting that the voice on the other end would be a delivery guy or the neighbor that continuously locked herself out of the building.

"Mr. Owen Parker sent me to come get you, ma'am. I have the car ready for you," answered a light masculine voice. I glanced down at my pajamas, and hit the talk button.

"Mr. Parker sent you? I'm not really ready." I was pretty sure my hair looked like a tornado had whipped across my pillow, and I hadn't even had my coffee yet.

"I can wait, ma'am. I was told to tell you to just wear something comfortable and to come as you are." The intercom crackled and I chewed my lip.

"I'll be down in a minute," I said into the speaker, and then hurried to find a pair of jeans. If Owen was going to have someone come get me first thing in the morning, then there was no way I was going to look my best. I did run a brush through my hair and swish some mouthwash before grabbing my purse and heading down.

Parked in front of my apartment building was a dark blue town-car with some sort of leaping creature as the hood ornament. I didn't know what kind of car it was, but I knew it was probably very expensive. As I opened the main entrance security door, I noticed the man standing in the entryway. He was a young and handsome in a crisp blue uniform.

"Ms. LaRue? If you'll follow me," he said courteously, leading me to the town-car. He opened the door and I slid across the heated leather seats. The car had that new car smell, and it was far nicer than any car I had ever been in. The man hopped in the driver's seat, and pulled out onto the road heading downtown.

"Where are you taking me? Is Owen here already?"

"Mr. Parker will be here this evening. Until then, he has arranged the day for you. Everything has been taken care of, and he would like you to enjoy yourself." The driver grinned at me as he turned on one of the side streets of downtown Des Moines and parked in front of a cute little brick building that housed the best spa in town. He ran around and opened my door, lending me a hand to step onto the street.

"Here we are, ma'am. Have a wonderful time."

"Thank you," I said, and he smiled as he jumped back in the car. It seemed a waste to have such a nice car hired for the five minute drive, but then again, Owen could afford it. The engine purred as the driver pulled away and I hurried out of the cold and into the warm building.

The door chimed softly as I stepped inside, my cheeks rosy. Soft classical music played overhead over the sound of the waterfall fountain in the corner. I had looked through the brochure for this place before, but I had never stepped inside. I had thought many a time of getting a massage here, but I could never seem to justify spending the money on myself.

"Kaylee! We thought you were going to sleep all day," Marissa shouted at me from across the room. Typical, boisterous Marissa. She sounded so loud in contrast with the quiet tranquility of the spa. I turned to see her and Allie sitting in white terrycloth robes sipping tea in comfortable looking chairs.

"What are you two doing here?" I asked, slightly confused as to why my two best friends would be sitting in a spa at eight in the morning waiting for me.

"Your new beau said you were getting pampered today and that we were invited to keep you company." Marissa grinned.

"Yup. He called and made sure we would come keep you entertained for the day until he got here. Is this the guy I saw give you flowers in the ambulance bay the other night? He's hot," Allie chimed in.

"And apparently loaded," Marissa added, gesturing to the room. She pushed a tendril of fiery red hair behind her ear and gave me a wicked grin. "He got a brother? I mean, I'd go for this Owen guy directly, but he seems pretty smitten with you. Plus, I like you too much to do that."

"Sorry, just a sister." I stood there looking at my friends, wondering just how Owen had known to invite these two women. Emma must have helped. "How long have you two been here?"

"Just long enough to put on these awesome robes. It's so soft, go gets yours quick. The massage lady is just getting the stones and the mud bath heated." Marissa leaned back and put her feet up on a stool. Allie pointed to a cute little door off to the side where I could put my things and change.

"He rented out the whole place just for the three

of us, so don't worry about taking up too much room. Marissa here used four cubbies," Allie said. She and Marissa had a cubbie battle going on at work, so it was no surprise that she would pick up on Marissa's tendency of using multiple cubbies.

Marissa rolled her eyes. "And why not?"

I left the two of them to banter back and forth about how many cubbies a person should reasonably use to store their things and stepped into the room to change. I could see Marissa had used the cubbies to organize her shoes, clothes, and purse, while Allie had neatly stowed all her things in a single spot. I shook my head, wondering how the three of us ever stayed friends, considering how different we all were. But perhaps it was because we were so different that we got along so well.

When I stepped out of the changing room, the massage therapist was waiting for me with a smile. She took the three of us back to a quiet room with three tables set up and instructed us each to lie down and relax. Allie giggled and hopped up on a table, Marissa and I right behind her. As the three of us slipped under warmed sheets, I grinned. This was going to be a fabulous day.

CHAPTER TWELVE

"There you go, honey, all done."

I turned my head from side to side in the mirror, barely recognizing myself. Marissa wolf-whistled and Allie clapped.

The hairdresser had piled my hair up on my head in such a way that it looked as though cascades of dark curls would fall endlessly down my back. I didn't even know how she made it look like my hair was that full and thick, but it was beautiful. My makeup was perfect, and it all accented the little black dress Owen had left at the spa for me to wear. Marissa had drooled as she looked at the designer label and threatened to steal it when I wasn't looking.

I felt like Cinderella.

"If you're Cinderella, what does that make us?

The ugly stepsisters?" Allie asked, sipping on a cup of tea. I hadn't realized I had said anything out loud.

"Yeah, and we don't even get to go the ball tonight!" Marissa added with a laugh. I blushed slightly, flustered.

"Oh, hey, speaking of which, here comes Prince Charming now," Allie announced, looking out the window to the street.

I looked in the mirror just in time to see Owen sauntering up to the glass door. He was wearing a casual gray suit and looked hot enough to start a fire. He looked so hot, I was surprised that there wasn't smoke drifting off of his footsteps.

He opened the door and glanced around until he saw me. His jaw dropped a little, and even in the reflection of the mirror, I could see his pupils dilate as I stood up to greet him. I hadn't gotten a reaction quite like that in a while. It made me feel all tingly and special.

"You look spectacular," he whispered, leaning forward to kiss my cheek gently, careful not to mess up my makeup. "Not that you don't usually look amazing, but...wow."

I laughed, glad to see him a little flustered. "Thank you."

"Well, ladies, thank you for keeping my date company today. I think it's time I stole her away, though," he said, managing to regain his composure as he turned towards Allie and Marissa.

"Thank you for the invite! We had a great time," Allie answered quickly. She grinned up at him.

"You sure you don't have a brother? Maybe a

cousin, even?" Marissa asked. Owen laughed. I was glad he was able to take her in stride. I loved Marissa, but she could be a bit much at first.

"You two have a great time. And remember to tell us all the good parts at work on Sunday," Marissa said with a wink. I could feel myself blush, but Owen just took my arm in his and grinned at her.

"I don't know if she'll have time to tell you all the good parts. Your shift is only twelve hours long after all." He winked at her and she lit up in a smile.

"I think you've got a keeper, Kaylee. Though, Owen, if it doesn't work out..." Marissa gave him a naughty smirk.

"Then I'll give Allie a call," he replied with a straight face. Allie snorted. He turned to me, his smile crinkling the corners of his eyes. "You ready?"

I nodded, and my friends waved goodbye as we stepped out the door. A limo pulled up to the curb as we stepped onto the sidewalk, and the driver hopped out to open the door. Owen let me slide in first, following closely behind me. The interior was warm and had romantic lighting.

"So where are we going?" I asked, excitement thrumming in my voice. This close to him, I could smell the soft scent of his cologne and his leg was warm against mine.

"You'll see. I want it to be a surprise. It's not far," he murmured as he leaned forward and kissed my cheek again.

The limo began to move. It went about three

blocks before it stopped again and the driver appeared at the door. I wondered just how many miles I was going to end up going in fancy cars today. I was guessing around three.

I stepped into the darkening evening, the cold air rushing up against my bare shoulders. We were in front of the Des Moines Botanical Gardens, the big glass dome glowing slightly from an inner light. Owen stepped out of the car and immediately shrugged out of his jacket and draped it across my shoulders without even waiting for me to get cold. It was warm and smelled like his cologne. I took a deep breath, my insides going tingly at being wrapped in his scent. He grabbed my hand, his body heat seeping into my palm, and pulled me toward the entrance.

He led me into the big dome housing all the tropical plants. I loved to come here during the winter to take a break from the gray Iowa cold and to be surrounded by heat and tropical flowers. It was usually busy as everyone else in Iowa typically had the same idea, but tonight, we had the place to ourselves.

By the waterfall in the center of the garden, a thick blanket was spread out along the floor with a full picnic dinner. Soft lighting gave the entire area a moonlit glow, the gurgling sounds of the waterfall filling the humid air. A small arrangement of plumeria flowers sat in the center of the blanket.

"This is amazing... how did you do this?" I asked. I had never heard of anyone renting the space for a private picnic.

He shrugged and smiled. "It wasn't hard. Here, come and have some dinner."

The blanket felt soft as I knelt down on the ground, settling my skirt modestly. Owen sat down smoothly next to me, our hands close enough to touch if we wanted them to.

Owen pulled four large mugs from the basket, followed by a big red thermos and then handed me a plate wrapped in tinfoil to open. He unscrewed the thermos and poured a steaming delicious red tomato soup into two of the cups, while I unwrapped the tinfoil. Inside were perfect grilled cheese triangles. As I looked at them, I realized that they weren't just plain grilled cheese, but stuffed with bacon, avocado, and at least two different kinds of cheese.

"Emma told you grilled cheese and tomato soup is my favorite, didn't she?" I asked with a grin. He stole a sheepish grin in my direction, as if he had been caught with his hand in the cookie jar.

"I really wanted you to like it. What do you think?"

"I love it." I loved that he was trying so hard to make me happy. It was incredibly endearing.

Owen grinned and pulled out a second thermos, this one in blue. He opened it and carefully poured a dark liquid into the remaining empty cups. The smell of rich hot chocolate made me smile, especially when he pulled out a can of Pringles potato chips.

"This I remembered on my own," he said with a small smile as he handed me the can. I smiled widely and popped the top, dunking a chip into my hot chocolate. Owen laughed at my enthusiasm and grabbed a chip for himself. He dipped it carefully, and stuck it in his mouth. A strange look came over his face. "This is seriously your favorite food?" he said around pieces of the chip still in his mouth.

I nodded and dipped another. He swallowed and looked at me as though I might be a little crazy. "You don't like it, do you?" I asked. He shook his head from side to side.

"It's, well," he paused. "It's disgusting."

"You just have no taste in good food," I teased him. He relaxed as he realized I wasn't going to hold his dislike against him. I knew that not everyone liked the sweet and salty combo.

"Right. I'll go tell the French chef that cooks for me that," he teased back.

"You have a French chef?"

He nodded like it was the most common thing in the world. He reached for a sandwich and bit into it carefully. When I was just talking with him, it was easy to forget that he was worth almost a billion dollars. "You'd like him. I don't know if he would appreciate the fine dining of potato chips and chocolate though."

"I saw chocolate covered Pringles in a store once. They were sold as a delicacy, so I'm pretty sure you just have wacky taste buds." I reached for a sandwich and dipped it in the tomato soup. It was a little slice of heaven, the cheese blending perfectly with the soup and accented by bacon. "I think I will never eat a plain grilled cheese again. This is amazing."

Owen grinned and reached for a second sandwich. "I thought you might like it. I had it this way in college, and I never looked back."

"I definitely like this version. Thank you. This whole day has been fantastic."

"You are most welcome. You look amazing, by the way." He set his hand on mine, sending a thrill through me. I blushed, but I didn't pull my hand away. In fact, I tipped my chin up and leaned forward, pressing my lips against his.

He tasted like grilled cheese, but I didn't care. He was delicious. Owen's hand went to the back of my head, his fingers tangling in my perfect curls as he pulled me closer. His tongue searched for mine, our mouths opening to find one another. He lowered his lips, his teeth grazing the tender skin of my jaw, sending heat surging through my belly.

"Do you have to catch a flight tonight?" I whispered, remembering the limo. I was giving serious contemplation to just taking him there on the blanket in the middle of the lush tropical garden, but having a bed would be better. He chuckled, the sound throaty and deep.

"No, no flight this time."

I looked up at him, biting my bottom lip with desire and just a touch of nerves. "You want to come back to my place?"

He kissed me again, taking my breath away. It was okay though, because when I was with him, I didn't need to breathe.

"We could do that. Or, I got us a hotel room."

"So you thought you were going to get lucky

tonight, huh?" I asked with a giggle, giving him a playful punch on the arm. He traced a finger down the curve of my cheek, the touch light but seductive.

"I suppose I should say I got myself a hotel room, but I made sure it would be big enough for two if you wanted to come visit." His eyes sparkled with amusement.

"Well, a hotel room would be nicer than my apartment. I didn't really clean this morning, so there would be dirty laundry all over the floor."

"Then perhaps we should put laundry all over the floor of the hotel room to make you feel more more at home," he whispered, leaning forward and kissing the curve where my jaw met my neck. I shivered with anticipation.

Owen stood up in one fluid motion, holding out his hand to help me up. Once I was on my feet, he pulled me into him, stealing a kiss. It was full of want, need, and pure desire. I couldn't have said no if I wanted to, though I really just wanted to scream yes.

We were back out to the limo in less than a minute, the driver waiting patiently at the door with the car. It was only a three minute drive to the downtown hotel, but I found myself unable to keep my fingers from unbuttoning his shirt. As he pushed my hands away, I looked up at him. "Sorry, they have a mind of their own, tonight."

When finally my fingers came to rest, they were on his tie. I contented myself with using it to pull him into me, kissing him with all my might until we got to the hotel room.

We bounded through the ornate lobby to a series of bronzed elevators that sent us whirring to the top floor. Owen was, of course, staying in the penthouse suite, but I barely looked at it as we stumbled into the bedroom.

Owen growled something, but I was too busy stripping to understand his words. I understood his meaning though. He was already hard, the bulge in his pants displaying exactly how much he wanted me. He kissed me, pushing me onto the bed.

"I want you so bad, Kaylee. You're the only thing I could think about all week." His voice was low and full of power. He was a man who could have anything he wanted, and he wanted me.

I shivered with anticipation, biting his lower lip as he tasted me. I felt my eyes roll to the back of my head as he began our night of pleasure, the bedsheets tangling around us as we writhed in ecstasy.

CHAPTER THIRTEEN

Three weeks later, after three more amazing dates, I was pretty sure I was in love. Owen Parker had successfully stolen my heart. We hadn't said anything yet, but I couldn't stop thinking about him. I looked forward to his phone calls, texts, and emails more than I looked forward to my days off.

We both wished we could have more time together, but with our crazy schedules and workloads, we were lucky to manage that many. I knew he had worked magic in order to make it out to Iowa as many times as he had. He took me to the symphony with a stop to a seafood restaurant for our first date, and the second was for ice cream and a movie, in which he rented the entire theater. The third date had been my favorite so far after the botanical gardens; he arranged a special backstage tour of the Des Moines Zoo. Watching him feed the penguins had kept me laughing for hours. Every one of the dates ended back in the penthouse suite, the two of us tangled up in the sheets.

It wasn't all happy though. While just thinking about him put a happy smile on my face and quickened my pulse, I wasn't sure what was going to happen next. We got along famously, but that was easy since we only saw each other once a week. The sex was fantastic, and I was falling hard for him, loving our dates and phone calls, but I was beginning to wonder if it would be enough. As much fun as we were both having, I couldn't see us continuing on like this for much longer. I didn't want this to end, but I didn't know how we could possibly keep our schedules and the distance from breaking us apart.

I glanced around my bedroom, mentally making sure I had everything. Owen was coming to visit, and I had packed a small bag of clothes and a toothbrush, actually planning ahead for once. I was tired of using my finger and his toothpaste to brush my teeth and having nothing clean to wear home. This time, I was going to be prepared for a stay at a hotel. I wasn't sure what adventure we were going to have on this trip, but I was prepared for anything.

My door buzzed, and I hurried downstairs, bag in hand. Owen was waiting patiently by the front door, leaning against the wall with his eyes closed. He smiled as soon as he heard the door open, and I hurried out to give him a kiss.

He looked exhausted. His normally crisp dress

shirt was wrinkled under his jacket, and he needed to shave. I looked closer and could see that his eyes were bloodshot, his lips and skin pale. I hoped he wasn't getting sick.

"Are you feeling okay?" I asked as he took my hand and we walked to his car. He no longer had us chauffeured around, instead preferring to drive us himself in a fancy sports car. Today's version was an Aston Martin.

"I'm just tired," he said with a sigh. "The flights were miserable getting out here and we kept getting delayed by weather. I know it's almost dinner time here, but my internal clock thinks it's closer to seven in the morning, and I've been up all night. I'm afraid I'm not going to be the best date tonight."

"Then how about we just have a quiet night in? We can lay in bed, eat pizza, maybe rent a movie? You can fall asleep, and we can just relax," I offered. He opened the car door for me to slide in, and he kissed me softly once I was seated.

"You're the best. That sounds fantastic."

It was a short drive to the hotel, and the staff recognized us as we made our way up the shiny elevators to his suite. I had offered to put him up at my place, but we both enjoyed room service too much to actually leave.

I set my toothbrush up in the bathroom, liking the way it looked next to Owen's. I sighed, though, seeing his travel kit sitting on the counter. Was it always going to be this way? Just one-night stays in hotels with days or even weeks in between visits? Owen had a long trip coming up, and I had barely managed to trade my shift to get the time off to see him this time. Working in a hospital meant that I had to work weekends and holidays, and Owen's travel schedule mandated that he leave for weeks at a time. His next trip was expected to take him out of the country to Dubai for at least three full weeks.

I came out of the bathroom to find Owen spread-eagle on the bed and snoring. He hadn't even managed to take off his shoes, their laces undone but still on his feet. I quietly tiptoed over and took his shoes off the rest of the way, then slid his pants off and unbuttoned his dress shirt. I pulled the sheets up to his chin, and he smiled in his sleep and snuggled into the soft material, drifting further into dreamland.

I slipped out of my clothes and into the silky nightgown I had brought, sliding under the sheets next to Owen. He mumbled something as he curled up on his side, his breathing deepening. I glanced at my watch-- six-thirty. My stomach grumbled and I glanced over at Owen. It was looking like this was going to be a very quiet date night indeed. I pulled out my phone and dialed for pizza, ordering a large Hawaiian style and a large pepperoni, then turning on the TV with subtitles and the volume all the way down. At least I could catch up on my TV.

Thirty minutes later, just as a new episode of some dancing show was starting, the pizza arrived. The scrawny pizza delivery boy eyed me in my sexy nighty, and I tried not to blush as I handed him the twenty dollar bill, then ducked back into the room. Just as I sat down to eat my pineapple and bacon deliciousness, my phone started to ring. I glanced at the caller ID and inwardly groaned. Work.

"This is Kaylee," I said softly, walking quickly to the bathroom so I wouldn't wake Owen. The door clicked gently behind me as my boss started begging.

"Kaylee, we are short-staffed, and I need you to come in. That stomach bug is going around, and I've had four people call in sick for tonight's shift. When can you get here?"

"I'm not coming in tonight. I'm sorry, but I have plans tonight," I told her. I knew she wasn't going to let me out of it that easily, though.

"Please, Kaylee, we're swamped. It'll be time and a half, and you only have to stay as long as we're busy," she pleaded into the phone. I knew that while I would get the extra pay, we would stay busy all night, especially if as many people had called in sick as she said. I could feel a guilt trip starting.

"No, I'm not coming in. Find someone else tonight. Liz is always looking to pick up shifts, try her," I told her getting ready to hang up.

"I did, and she's sick too. Please, Kaylee, I'm desperate."

I wavered for a moment. Owen was fast asleep and not likely to wake up at all this evening. I was just watching bad TV and eating pizza; maybe I could help them out, at least for a couple hours. I bit my tongue as the habit to take as many shifts as possible tried to make me say yes. I was supposed to be with Owen tonight. I heard the bed creak in the other room, and I forced the "yes" creeping up my throat back down. He had flown out to see me, not to have me run off to work while he slept.

"I can't." I tried my best to make it sound final.

"Kaylee, please. At least just see if you can come in for a couple hours," my boss implored into the phone. I felt bad, especially since all I was doing was watching him sleep. I knew my coworkers would be struggling with the short staff, and I hated to leave them in the lurch. I could feel my loyalties straddling a fence, and I hated it. I was going to feel guilty no matter what decision I made.

"I can't. I'm sorry," I said quickly and hung up the phone. I knew she was going to call me back eventually, but for the moment I was safe. I set the phone down and turned on the sink, splashing some cold water on my face. I hated feeling like I was letting someone down.

I dried my face and stepped out to the main room to find Owen sitting up in the bed. He had dark circles under his eyes, but he was awake and looking at me.

"I flew out here to be with you," he said softly. I frowned, confused. I seemed to remember telling my boss no.

"That's why I told them no."

"You took an awful long time to do it."

"What's that supposed to mean?" I asked, surprised at his tone. He must still be half-asleep and cranky, but I didn't like where he was heading.

"I flew over twelve hours to get here, but you gave serious thought to going to work." A touch of anger entered his voice. I took a deep breath, reminding myself that he had been up all night.

"I did think about it. I thought about going in and helping my coworkers, people who I consider my friends, while you were busy sleeping. I didn't though. I'm staying here." I moved to the foot of the bed in order to see him better. The TV cast a strange bluish glow on his skin, his hair poking up in an unruly pattern. He looked like he could fall over and go straight back asleep at any moment, except for the frown on his face keeping him awake.

"I don't appreciate that you even considered it," he said quietly.

"You mean you're mad that I considered doing something while you were sleeping?" I crossed my arms and frowned at him. He ran a hand through his hair, the TV light casting a strange assortment of shadows.

"I don't get to see you very often, and I'm leaving on a long trip. I didn't think you would run off in the middle of the night." His voice was quiet, like the calm before a thunderstorm.

"So I can't leave to go to my job for three hours, but you can leave for three weeks for yours." The words were out of my mouth before I could stop them. Owen's eyes went wide and then narrowed.

"That's not fair. My job is about the travel. I don't have a choice. I flew three extra hours just to get here, to see you. But you go do your oh-so-important extra shift, and I'll just sit here by myself. If I had known that you didn't want to stay with me tonight, I would have just stayed in New York."

"Hey, I'm not going in to work! How many times do I have to tell you that I told them no?" I could hear my voice rising with every word, a hot anger beginning to boil in my stomach.

Owen's shoulders sagged and weariness weighed on his body. "I'm sorry, Kaylee. I'm just exhausted, and I hate that I'm sleeping through our date night. This isn't what I had planned."

I sat gingerly on the edge of the bed, an hollow dread replacing the anger I felt. "Is it always going to be like this? Just random meetings in hotel rooms where we both are fighting with our schedules?"

Owen stared at the sheets in his lap, his brow furrowed. "I don't know, but I don't like how hard it is right now. I hate that I'm not going to see you for three weeks, and then who knows when we'll have more than a day together again."

I bit my lip and tried not to focus on the thick feeling growing in the back of my throat. I played with the cuticle on my thumb, the words coming out slow. "This isn't going to work between us, is it?"

Owen didn't answer. His hair was across his eyes, obscuring his face, but his silence was all I needed to know the answer. Our worlds had collided, but they weren't meant to stay that way. Despite the feelings I had for him, our lives were just too different and too far apart for us to be together. Sure, we could keep trying, but at what cost? Eventually his traveling and my hospital schedule would just be too much to fight against and it would blow up in our faces. Better to end it now, when it wouldn't hurt quite so much. I knew the lie as soon as I thought it. It would hurt more than anything.

"I'll get my things," I said quietly, standing from the bed. His hand shot out and grabbed mine, keeping me near him.

"No, Kaylee. Don't go. Don't ever go." His voice was soft in the darkness. I realized I was trembling.

"Owen..."

"I love you, Kaylee." He said it simply, his voice soft. I felt my heart forget to beat. It no longer needed to. It didn't beat for me anymore anyway; it beat for Owen.

"I love you too, Owen." The words flowed out easily, my heart overjoyed. They were truer than anything I had ever said in my life. I really did love him.

"Come with me."

"What? What do you mean?" I sat back down. Owen's eyes were bright, a smile beginning to form around the edges of his mouth.

"Come with me on this business trip."

"I can't. You know I can't," I said, shaking my head.

"Why?" His eyes searched mine. "Money? Not a problem. Work? You can get the time off. Come travel with me. I'll even talk to your boss. I'm sure you can get the time off if I made a sizable donation to the hospital."

Fear lurched in my stomach. "I can't."

He peered at me, his eyes hopeful. "Why, Kaylee?"

I picked furiously at the cuticle on my thumb. If

I kept this up it would bleed, but I didn't care. I took a shaky breath, embarrassed and afraid to tell him. "I hate flying. And I'm not good in strange places."

"You flew to Emma's wedding," he said encouragingly.

"Because it was her *wedding*. You don't even want to know what it took to get me through the flight." That hot sticky feeling was growing in the back of my throat and I swallowed hard. I didn't want to cry.

"We can work around that. At least think about it. We could be together this way." I could hear the excitement in his voice, and I wanted to feel it too. I wanted to be with him. I just didn't want to leave Iowa to do it. I nodded, though.

"I'll think about it."

Thunder rumbled, and I heard a splash of rain hit the window as a storm rolled in. Owen grinned at me, hope and excitement radiating from him. I knew I wasn't going to really have to think about it. For the chance to be with Owen, for the chance to make this relationship work, I would get on a plane. I'd become a flipping flight attendant if it meant I could be with Owen.

"I'll try it. But you're going to have to have some serious alcohol on the flight."

Owen's face lit up the room, and he pulled me into the bed with him. As he kissed me, I knew I could do this. As much as I hated flying and traveling, I would give it a chance for Owen. For this.

Rain hit the window harder as Owen kissed me. I

could do this. I could do anything if I was with Owen. He wrapped his arms around me, the heat of his skin comforting as we nestled back into the sheets. He was back asleep in minutes, his breathing deep and even. Thunder rattled the windows, but he didn't stir as the rain pounded against the glass outside. It was as if the rain was washing away my worries, bringing change and something new.

CHAPTER FOURTEEN

I took a deep breath and closed my eyes. I could do this.

Owen squeezed my hand reassuringly, and I gave him a nervous smile. The plane moved forward and my hand clamped down on his. I could do this.

When Emma had told me that her wedding would be in the Caribbean, I almost didn't go. But she was my sister, so I had dutifully started working on overcoming my fear of flying. I bought books, listened to 'get over your fear' programs on tape, I even met with a hypnotherapist. In the end, the only thing that had gotten me through that flight was a bottle of whiskey.

The plane began to speed up, the small private jet starting its sprint down the runway. I could feel the plane star to vibrate, the hum of the engines drowning out all other noise. I wanted to scream for it to stop, but I was determined to do this. I held Owen's hand in a death grip. I was pretty sure when we got off the plane that he was going to need X-rays and a cast. That was, of course, if he even managed to have a hand left, on account of the way I was squeezing. He just smiled at me and let me keep tightening my grip.

In deep, out slow. In deep, out slow. I was resolute not to use the little pills in my pocket. I could do this. *Just don't concentrate on the plane.* It seemed as though the plane was getting smaller, and I could feel the miles of empty space increasing beneath me. It was such a long, long way down.

"Just think of it like being in a car," Owen said, leaning over to kiss my cheek. He leaned back in his leather seat, looking far too at ease for being suspended in a tin can a mile above the ground.

"Right. A car. Just a really weird car," I said through gritted teeth. My jaw was going to hurt tomorrow. This was just a quick flight to New York. We were leaving a little early so I could spend some time with Emma in the city before we took the long flight to Dubai. I had no idea how I was going to survive.

"Something to drink?" a stewardess asked, her blue uniform crisp and perfect. I wondered if she liked her job. I wouldn't have.

"Vodka, please. A big shot of vodka," Owen told her. "And an iced tea for me, please."

The stewardess smiled warmly and placed a hand

on Owen's shoulder as she walked past. I didn't even care. If she brought me the vodka and we didn't die on this plane, she could kiss him. She returned in a moment, a tall glass of tea for Owen and a nice tumbler of clear liquid for me. She even brought a little bottle of cranberry juice.

"Here you go. Let me know if you need anything else," she said, handing me the drinks. I took a big gulp, feeling it burn down my esophagus. I could do this, and a little liquid courage would help.

"You're doing great," Owen said as he sipped on his iced tea. I envied how he could look so relaxed on this flying death trap. "We'll be there in two and a half hours."

"Right. Because that's practically no time at all."

"Have another drink." He kissed my cheek and turned on the TV across from us. A castle and music I recognized instantly filled the screen. "And something to keep you entertained."

I couldn't help but grin as the animated movie from my childhood started. I sipped on my drink, feeling slightly more relaxed as I hummed along with the opening credits. A bright side occurred to me about flying. I could sing along with the movie, and the noise of the engines would drown out my lack of vocal abilities.

I could do this.

***

I peeked open an eye, the light sending a sliver of pain directly into my head. I knew I shouldn't have had that second drink. My stomach rolled, promising me that if I moved, whatever was left in it would come up. As if there were anything even left in it after we landed.

"Hey, Sleeping Beauty," a soft female voice called to me. I pouted, wanting to throw a pillow at the voice, but I knew the motion would just make everything hurt again. "Here have some of this."

I felt a glass press up against my lips and I unhappily opened my mouth, letting a dribble of lemon flavored drink in. If I could keep that down, I knew I would be a happier camper. Keyword being "if."

"Where am I?" I croaked. My throat felt like fire. I was never drinking again.

"Owen's hotel room. You have got to remember to eat before you drink next time," Emma answered. "Here, have another sip."

I sat up slowly and took the glass from her. She looked far too perky and pleasant. I gave her a dirty look as I took a bigger gulp of the drink. It was at least making me feel more awake.

"What time is it?" I asked, glancing around the room. I sat in the middle of a king-sized bed surrounded by puffy pillows. The drapes were thankfully pulled shut, but I could imagine giant glass windows or a balcony behind them. I would have liked it if my stomach didn't feel like a tiny alien might pop out of it at any second.

"A little after ten in the morning. Though, that's Eastern Time, so it'll feel earlier for you."

"Why did you wake me up?" I growled. I just

wanted to dive back under my sheets and never move again. Maybe I would bring some of this magic drink with me, though.

"Because, we have stuff to do today. Remember, we made plans?"

I groaned. Emma wanted to show me the city, and we were supposed to go out shopping in true New York style with Rachel. I silently cursed the flight attendant and her crisp uniform for bringing me the second tumbler of vodka.

"Get up. You aren't that hung-over," Emma said, nudging me gently.

"Yes, I am," I fired back. She laughed and stood up from the bed.

"Drink that up. I'll start a shower for you and get some breakfast up here. We are going to have fun today."

I groaned again and slumped back down into the pillows. It was going to be a long day.

***

Whatever drink Emma had given me had worked miracles. The shower definitely helped, and the toast she forced down my throat probably did something too. By the time we were in the lobby, I only had a slight headache and thought my stomach should stay put for the rest of the day. As we exited the elevator, a well-dressed woman in her mid-forties hurried over to meet us.

"Hi, Rachel, sorry we're late. Rough flight last night," Emma greeted her.

"No problem at all," Rachel said with a smile. "It's nice to see you again, Kaylee. If we're ready, Dean has the car just outside."

The three of us exited the hotel room, the sky heavy with an impending rainstorm. Waiting by the curb was a sleek SUV with tinted windows. Rachel slid into the front seat, and Emma and I took the back. There was an unspoken tension between Rachel and Dean, but I couldn't figure out if they were fighting love or just plain fighting.

"Kaylee, you remember Dean?" Emma asked, gesturing toward the driver. An athletic-looking man sat in the front seat, his dark hair peppered with gray. He turned around and grinned, reaching a hand back to shake mine.

"I'm glad to see Emma finally got you out of bed. We have some shopping for you ladies to do," he said with a grin. Dean merged the car effortlessly out into the heavy New York traffic. A thunderstorm warning for later in the day came across the radio, but Dean turned it down and flipped on some light music. I kept my nose pressed to the glass, trying to absorb the whole city from the car window. Before, I had been a little too wasted to notice just how big everything was on my way in.

The city buildings rose up, reaching past where I could see, monsters of gray stone and cement. Well-dressed people hurried back and forth on the busy streets, everyone doing their best to ignore everyone else. It was so different from home. I was glad I didn't have to drive, as cars ducked and weaved around us, Dean managing to slide into spaces I never would have tried for. I think there were more cars on this one street than there were in the whole city of Des Moines.

"How do you live here, Emma?" I asked as we stopped for traffic. The street looked like sales lot for used cars than a means of travel.

"What? The traffic?" She shrugged. "I guess I've gotten used to it. The city seemed so big and strange at first, but now, I kind of like it."

"I don't think I could ever get used to this." The city was just too big and too busy for me. Give me my quiet Midwestern city over this any day. Not that it wasn't impressive, it just wasn't something I wanted to live in.

Dean navigated the SUV down another street, merging through a sea of bright yellow taxi cabs to pull up in front of a stylish brick building. A big glass window held mannequins in graceful poses, their clothes perfect and beautiful to the point where I thought they might come alive and coax us to buy their wares. Rachel led Emma and me inside while Dean waited with the car.

The store was quiet except for soft music playing overhead. I wondered where all the customers were as Rachel headed deeper into the shop. She and Emma both seemed to know where they were going so I followed, glancing at the beautiful items for sale.

A dark red purse caught my eye, and I stopped to pick it up. It was a beautiful little creation, the leather a deep wine red. I even recognized the designer label. I looked at the price tag, knowing I had a little money saved up and could splurge on a purse, especially if I could say I got it in New York City. $2,290.00. I didn't have that much to splurge. I set it carefully back down and hurried to catch up with Rachel and Emma.

I found them in a private area, Rachel deep in conversation with a saleswoman. As I walked up, Rachel turned and grinned.

"I went ahead and picked some things out for you to try. They're in that dressing room there." Rachel pointed to one of the large changing rooms. I smiled weakly. If the clothes were half as expensive as the purse, there was no way I could even afford to be in the same room as the clearance rack.

Emma must have read my mind, as she quickly added, "Don't look at the price, Kaylee. This is my treat for you. I never thought I would get you out to New York, so I'm excited to spoil you a little."

I almost told her no. I almost said that she shouldn't spend that kind of money. Then I remembered who she was married to, and the words died before they made it out of my mouth. Jack made enough money to buy that purse before he got out of bed in the morning.

I walked confidently into the changing room and slid on the first pair of pants. They were a soft tan color and made of a light linen material. I was shocked at how well they fit. Rachel was a great judge of size. I turned in the mirror and was pleased with what I saw.

"Told you those would look good on her," Emma

said to Rachel as I stepped out. Rachel nodded.

"You are getting better. Soon, you'll be dressing me!" Rachel said. The two of them laughed before Rachel stood to get a closer look at the pants. "Those will be great for you in Dubai," Rachel said. She came up and had me spin. "Lightweight, but full length. Mr. Parker suggested we pick some things up for you to wear on your trip."

I blushed a little. I had no idea what to pack for two weeks in the Middle East. I almost brought only shorts and tank-tops for the desert heat before remembering that the local populace probably would prefer that I wore something a little less revealing. My suitcase was sadly light as the majority of my clothes were scrubs from work.

"Go in and try on the purple shirt with those slacks," Emma said. She was practically bouncing in her seat. I gave her a strange look.

"Since when did *you* get interested in clothes?" I asked her. When we were living in the same house, I never worried about her stealing my clothes because she just wore the same jeans and T-shirt every day. She gave me a proud smile.

"Rachel's been training me. She's actually managed to show me the error of my ways and teach me something that resembles a fashion sense."

Rachel blushed. "You picked it up pretty quickly. I'll have you designing your own clothes any day now."

This time Emma flushed. "No way."

"I'm going to have to agree with her, Rachel. You should have seen the scarf she tried to knit.

And the teddy bear she made in home economics. Well, I'm not sure you could even properly call it a bear."

Emma blushed almost purple. "It wasn't pretty. Nightmarish things happen when I try to sew."

"Hmm, I guess that's job security for me," Rachel said with a chuckle. I ducked into the changing room and threw on the purple shirt. It was just a silk button-up blouse, but I could imagine it doing well in the desert heat. I stepped out and did a little catwalk.

"I like it, but not with those pants," Rachel said with a laugh as I struck a model pose. Emma nodded.

"Maybe with a khaki skirt?" Emma's face became thoughtful.

"Or the black slacks," Rachel mused aloud. I grinned. It was fun letting them play dress-up with me. The clothes were all so beautiful that I was having fun just trying them on. Knowing that they would make sure I was dressed perfectly made it easy to try on things that I would never pick out myself.

We went through mountains of clothes, loading the salesperson who came to check on us with piles of rejects. She didn't mind, though, as the piles of things we were purchasing continued to grow. I had clothes for my trip, and even a new dress to wear out while with Owen that night.

When we finally walked out of the store, I didn't even want to look at the bill. I had seen price tags of over two grand on some of the dresses that Emma wanted to buy me, and the idea of seeing the final number higher than my yearly salary was just too intimidating. I knew if I saw that, I would never wear them for fear of ruining them.

Rachel grinned at me as we headed back out to the waiting car. I could see why Emma loved Rachel. The two of them, despite their age difference, got along famously.

"You lovely ladies have a wonderful time and spend all of Mr. Saunders' money?" Dean asked as we piled back into the SUV.

"Every dime. But Kaylee is going to look fab-u-lous!" Emma said, rocking her shoulders and giving her hand a single wave. Rachel snorted, and Dean just rolled his eyes as he pulled out into traffic.

I gave her a playful shove, but I couldn't wait to show Owen what we had bought.

CHAPTER FIFTEEN

I stood, anxiously waiting for Owen in the lobby of the hotel where we were staying. Since he traveled on such a regular basis, he didn't bother keeping a house in the city and instead just rented the penthouse suite whenever he needed it. He had told me to meet him in the lobby, and he would pick me up when he finished a meeting with Jack to go over the details for his upcoming business trip. He had told me he was taking me to a fancy French restaurant and to get dolled up.

I fussed with the straps on my dress, as much making sure that it was in place as giving my hands something to do. Rachel and Emma had found me the perfect dress while we were out shopping, and then Rachel arranged for someone to come to the hotel to do my hair and makeup for my date. I chewed my lip, knowing that I was probably smearing my lipstick. Owen was only a few minutes late, but because of my dress, everyone who walked through the lobby stopped to look at me.

I looked like something off the red carpet at the Oscars. I wore a long, flowing gown of soft white fabric that fluttered when I walked. It was cut in a Grecian style, with a form fitting top and a skirt that cascaded beautifully to pool on the floor. The dress was long enough that I was able to wear simple white ballet slippers, the skirt's hem long enough that my feet were completely hidden. My hair was slightly pulled back out of my face, but left loose down my back in soft waves. Emma lent me a simple diamond necklace and sparkling chandelier earrings to complete the look.

Owen finally walked in through the front door, moving the crowd aside like he owned the place. Our eyes met across the lobby, and he moved toward me, slicing through the room as though it were empty. His dark gray suit somehow made his eyes even bluer as he smiled at only me.

"You look better every time you put on a dress," he said as soon as he reached me. I kissed him gently, not wanting to leave a lipstick mark. He took my hand and held me out as though we had just finished dancing, his eyes going up and down, appraising the dress. He held my hand up over my head, coaxing me into a spin. The fabric floated gracefully before settling again. "I think this is my favorite dress I've seen you in."

"Thank you," I said, blushing to the roots of my

hair. "You look pretty good yourself."

He grinned and did a model spin for me, finishing with a flamboyant hand on his hip. Even with his goofy antics, he looked hot. The dark gray of the suit stood out against the white of a dress shirt, and a tie the exact color of his eyes pulled everything together. The suit accented his broad shoulders and tapered waist, even showing off his perfect ass.

A camera flashed and I remembered that we weren't in our private hotel suite, but instead in the lobby of a very stylish and popular hotel. A woman in a wide brimmed hat and oversized sunglasses looked at us with wide eyes.

"Are you two celebrities? I hear celebrities stay here," the woman babbled, her eyes excited as she held up her camera to take another picture.

"No, we're just normal people." Owen said as he smiled politely at the tourist. She looked disappointed, and she turned to walk away. I giggled, the idea of being mistaken for a celebrity amusing me. No one at home would ever mistake me for a movie star. Owen carefully folded my hand into the crook of his arm, and escorted me out to a waiting car.

I had given up on trying to figure out what expensive model of car we were driving. Owen seemed to enjoy having a new fancy car at every opportunity. He had told me he didn't actually own any of them, he just rented whatever he felt like when he needed one. I had laughed at the idea that I actually owned more cars than a billionaire, since I actually did own a car, but then he pointed out that he owned a plane. I told him planes didn't count as cars, so I still had more.

This one was a silver convertible. It was early afternoon, and sunshine peeked through the clouds, casting a warm, dappled light across the city. The weather was finally nice enough that a convertible sounded wonderful. Owen opened the door to the passenger side, his face going pale as I sat down.

"I just realized your hair, and the car..."

I laughed. "Don't worry. There is enough hair spray on this to hold it through a hurricane. Besides, I think the windswept look is in right now. I'd rather drive with the top down and enjoy this weather than have the roof up."

His face brightened again, and he jumped into the driver's seat. With a roar of the engine, he pulled out onto the busy street, the wind blowing gently in my hair. He drove through the city, pointing out different landmarks and places that he thought I might enjoy. It wasn't long before we reached a stylish white brick building with ivy crawling up toward the windows.

Owen tossed the keys to a valet and hurried over to help me out. I smoothed my hair from the drive, a little surprised at just how well it had held up. It was surprisingly easy to maneuver out of the fancy sports car in my flowing dress, but I gladly accepted Owen's hand to help me stand. Any excuse to touch him was a good excuse.

Inside the white building, we walked through the main room to a private dining area. Everything had a golden glow, as though the entire place was candlelit. A string quartet played softly in the corner, their music soothing and the perfect volume for dinner conversation.

Owen pulled an ornate chair out for me to get my legs situated under the heavy wooden table, and then helped to push me under once I was seated. I glanced nervously at the array of utensils displayed before me. I was used to a salad fork and regular fork at restaurants, but there were tiny forks, an extra spoon, and more glasses than I knew what to do with. I was out of my league here.

The waiter placed my napkin on my lap and handed me a large leather-bound menu as Owen ordered a bottle of wine. I opened it up, wondering what culinary delights I would find inside. Instead, I stared at the pages, feeling foolish. I couldn't understand a word on the menu. It was all in French, and despite my French last name, I couldn't read a word.

Owen peeked over his menu at me and caught my blank look. He whispered softly, "Chicken, fish, or beef?"

"Fish."

"Do you mind if I order for you?"

I shook my head, grateful that I wouldn't have to choose between butchering the beautiful language or pointing to the menu in silent shame.

"Is there anything you don't want to eat? Are you all right trying escargot? It's amazing here," Owen asked. I smiled, glad he was making sure I would enjoy what he ordered for me.

"I'll try anything. Escargot is snails, right? I'll try it, but I have no idea how to actually eat it." I gave him a brave smile, a touch of nerves hitting me. This place was far fancier than anything I had ever even imagined possible. Back home, even the nicest places let people walk in and order wearing jeans and a T-shirt. Here, everyone was elegantly dressed in designer gowns and suits, and I had a feeling that jeans and a T-shirt would never even get to look at a menu.

When the waiter returned to fill up our wine glasses, Owen ordered in perfect, or at least what sounded perfect to me, French. The waiter nodded and took our menus, disappearing once again.

"You speak French?" I asked Owen, impressed at learning of his talent. He blushed a little.

"Only enough to sound like I know what I'm doing when I order in a restaurant. Pierre, my chef, taught me a little. I can swear decently in French, though, also thanks to Pierre." He gave me a little boy's naughty grin and I couldn't help but smile back.

"What other languages do you speak?" I sipped on my wine, wondering if I should raise my pinky in the air. No, that was for tea; it just didn't seem fancy enough to just drink the normal way in a place like this.

"I am getting pretty good at Arabic, and I can order cervezas like a pro in Spanish. But other than that, I just know key phrases. You?"

"I know some medical Spanish, but I wouldn't say I'm even close to fluent. Will I need to know

Arabic for our trip?"

Owen smiled and shook his head. "No. All these business dealings will be done in English."

I was about to ask more, but the waiter returned with two small round plates that he set in front of each of us. Six tan and white shells were presented like artwork, each in its own little hollow of the special plate and dressed in butter. It smelled fantastic.

Owen picked up a pair of tongs and a slender two pronged fork from the assortment of utensils before us. I mimicked his motions as he grasped the shell with the tongs and used the fork to pull the meat out of the shell. I hesitantly put the food in my mouth, unsure of what to expect.

It was delicious. The snail reminded me slightly of an oyster, but with an earthy taste instead of salty. The butter sauce was creamy and divine, giving the little piece of meat more flavor than I had been expecting for something so small.

"You like it?" Owen asked, dipping a piece of bread into the butter sauce.

I nodded, going for a second shell. The tongs slipped and the shell threatened to fly off the table, like the scene from *Pretty Woman*, but I caught it before it got too far.

"Slippery little suckers," I said, glancing around to make sure no one else had seen my scramble with the shell. Owen chuckled.

"You'll get better at it the more you eat them."

"I know we are going to Dubai, but what are we doing there? Are you sure it will be okay for me to come?" I half hoped he would tell me that I actually wasn't coming and that I didn't have to get on another plane. I half hoped that I could just rent a car and drive home, but that would mean I wouldn't be with Owen.

"Yes, I'm sure that it's fine. I wouldn't have asked you otherwise. I know you had to take time off work for this, which I appreciate, so I'm going to make sure you have a good time. As far as what we are doing there, we will be wooing a sheik."

"A sheik? Like a prince?" I sat up straighter at the table. I never thought I would meet royalty. The waiter came and whisked the empty escargot dishes away, placing a small bowl of sorbet in front of me. I looked up at Owen, confused as to why dessert was being served.

"It's a palate cleanser before the main course," he explained.

I nodded and took a taste. Sweet orange sorbet.

"So a sheik, huh?" The sorbet was gone in two bites. I hoped dinner was coming soon, because despite the escargot and now the sorbet, I was still hungry.

"Yes. Sheik al-Saffar owns a large portion of the oil fields in production currently. He is thinking of partnering with Jack's company, due in part to Jack's marketing success. My job is to convince him that, since I am the head of marketing, my team will sell his oil better than he can himself." Owen folded his hands neatly on the table in front of him as though he had just finished a business proposal. I leaned back thoughtfully in my seat.

"I have a feeling it's more complicated than that, isn't it?"

"You might have a future in this business, Kaylee," he said, a grin breaking across his face.

"Nah, I'm better suited to scrubs than suits."

The waiter returned, refilling our wine glasses and placing the main course on the table. I almost didn't want to eat it because it was so pretty. A small fillet of white fish sat perched on a bed of onion, fennel, and tomatoes with a sauce that I could only describe as heavenly. Small clams and shrimp dotted the plate, adding to the amazing sauce. I had heard the word *bouillabaisse* when Owen had ordered and was sure that was what the sauce was called. I could die happy if I only ate that for the rest of my life.

Owen smiled at my look of rapture as I tasted the food before he continued. "We are meeting with the sheik and his son to forge a personal relationship with them. A lot of these business deals are built more on whom you like than what you can do. Most companies can offer similar services, but what they can't do is the relationship. The sheik actually had an arrangement with one of our competitors, but he wasn't getting what he wanted, so he has come to us. We offer almost the exact same core services, but we are willing to give him that something extra he is looking for."

"So, *you* are the sales pitch, then. The relationship that he is looking for. He wants someone he likes to sell his oil for him."

Owen nodded, a smile spreading across his face.

"You're getting it."

We sat quietly for a moment, each of us enjoying our food. Owen gave me a bite of his beef bourguignon, and I shared my fish with him. I was hungrier than I thought, because despite my best efforts, the fish was gone long before I was full.

"Earlier, you said, 'We are wooing'. Do you mean me, or the company?"

"You, actually. You will be able to help me quite a bit with this."

My forehead crinkled as I tried to figure out how I would be able to help. I was a medical professional, not a salesperson. Especially not an oil markets salesperson. Unless the sheik needed help controlling his cholesterol or fixing a broken leg, I couldn't see what use I was going to be.

Owen smiled at me, waiting for the waiter to serve the next part of our meal before answering. A small plate of different kinds of cheese sat between us, waiting to be shared. I tried them cautiously, but found their flavors were actually quite good.

"I have been invited to dinner with the sheik and his son, and was told to bring a guest. It is very common to discuss business matters over dinner, and as I am trying to forge a more personal relationship with him, this is the perfect opportunity to bring you along. If it goes well, there will be more dinners. More dinners means more opportunities to impress him." Owen watched my face carefully, gauging my reaction to his words.

"I'm not sure I'm going to be very good at this, Owen. I'm not good at selling things," I said softly.

"I was the kid in elementary school whose parents ended up buying subscriptions to ten magazines and paying for entire boxes of candy bars because I couldn't get anyone else to buy them."

"Kaylee, you are beautiful and smart. You're easy to talk to and you can carry a conversation. You're perfect for this." Owen reached out and touched my hand, his confidence in me surging through our skin. I felt my cheeks redden at the compliments.

"Thank you. I just don't want to embarrass you. Or Jack's company."

"You could never embarrass me," Owen said softly, his eyes intent on mine. I felt another blush sear through my cheeks.

The waiter returned and Owen released my hand. The empty cheese plate was taken away and replaced with dessert and cups of coffee. A dark chocolate torte with a raspberry glaze for me and a deceptively simple peach tart for Owen sat like presents before us. I'm pretty sure I died and went to heaven with the first bite, and then again with every bite after.

"I'll do my best with the sheik, but I can't make any promises," I told Owen once the dessert was gone. I seriously considered licking my plate but decided that I was in too nice of a place to do so.

"I just want you to be you, Kaylee. I know you are going to be amazing," Owen said, his voice full of trust. I smiled and sipped on my coffee, a little nervous. I didn't want to let him down.

"If this all goes well, it would be really good for

Jack's company, wouldn't it?" I asked.

Owen nodded. "It would be huge. I mean, Jack's company is already successful, but this would increase our market share by another third."

I felt a pressure settle on my shoulders. I knew that this was not my responsibility, but I wanted to make sure I helped Owen as much as possible. I was going to be the perfect dinner guest, even if I had to fake every word. I wasn't going to let Owen down.

"Brandy or cognac, mademoiselle?"

I startled slightly at the waiter's question, lost deep in my thoughts of being a good dinner guest.

"Cognac, please." I glanced at Owen and he hid a smile at my startle.

"Thinking much?" he chided softly. I stuck my tongue out at him before I remembered that we were at a very fancy restaurant.

"Just trying to figure out some witty banter for the sheik."

"Don't think too hard." Owen sipped at his own cognac, the corners of his mouth twitching with amusement. I wanted to stick my tongue out at him again, but I refrained this time. Barely.

"I guess I just need someone to practice my witty banter with. Maybe I can get that waiter to come back," I teased, pretending to look around for the waiter.

Owen chuckled softly; I loved that noise. It was a masculine laughter that suited him so well. I could listen to him laugh like that all day.

CHAPTER SIXTEEN

"You want to take a walk around the park?" Owen asked when we returned to the hotel. I glanced up at the darkening sky, then out toward the trees. Green sprouts were just starting to form on the bare branches, in wait of spring showers to nourish them. The sky was dark, but it still looked like we had some time before the rain would hit.

"Sure," I answered. Owen grinned, and grabbed my hand and the two of us practically skipped hand in hand into the park. We found a path that meandered through the trees, the two of us just quietly taking it all in. From the corner of my eye I could see his bodyguard shadowing us silently. I ignored him, instead just focusing on being with Owen. I loved the way his hand felt in mine--strong and warm, protective and secure. I loved the way he smelled like a clear spring in winter and the way he wrapped me up in his arms. Just thinking of being held in his arms made me squeeze his hand a little tighter, glad just to be with him.

A hot dog stand resided off the path, a bright yellow umbrella over a light brown cart. The smell of cooking meat wafted through the air, and even though we had just finished a satisfying gourmet meal, my stomach rumbled. Owen gave me a surprised look at how loudly my stomach had growled.

"You hungry?" he asked.

"Maybe a little. I didn't eat much today, so even though the food was amazing, the serving size was a little small," I said sheepishly. Owen squeezed my hand.

"I can go for a snack myself. I've never eaten there, but it is supposed to be the fanciest place in town, so I thought I should take you. You deserve the best."

A flood of warm fuzzies flowed through me at his words. No only did he love me, he really liked me too.

"Can I buy you a hot dog?" I asked as Owen's stomach growled in response to mine.

"You don't have to buy me a hot dog. I'll get it. I don't know if you know this, but I'm kind of rich," he whispered theatrically in my ear as we approached the small stand. I gave him a playful push, pulling out some money from inside my dress. Owen raised his eyebrow as he looked down the top of my dress to where I had stashed my ID and a little money.

"I know, but you bought dinner. Let me get the hot dogs."

"Like I can say no to you anyway," he said, shaking his head with a good-natured laugh.

I paid the man for two hot dogs, and together we ate them as we walked through the park. Owen pretended to bump into me as we walked, and I bumped back into him, both of us laughing under our breath as we tried to maintain the illusion that it was always an accident.

Thunder rumbled, and Owen turned us back toward the hotel. The clouds overhead were starting to get darker and more angry looking by the minute. I wasn't sure just how much longer they were going to hold back before letting loose.

We had just passed by the hot dog stand again when a crack of thunder made me jump. Owen laughed and pulled me close to him, draping his arm around my shoulder. I smiled up at him and felt something wet land on my cheek. I touched it with my fingertips, confused for a moment until a second heavy drop landed square on my nose. Owen and I looked right at one another with realization that it was raining just as the down pour started.

It was as if someone had turned on the shower faucet, the rain starting quicker than either of us could have expected. We ran for the nearest trees, but their bare branches offered no protection from the sudden deluge. I shivered, the two of us already completely soaked by the sudden microburst. Owen quickly shrugged out of his jacket and wrapped it around my shoulders, the satin inside still warm from his body.

I reached up, wrapping my hand around the back of his neck and pulling him down for a kiss. Our lips met, the taste of the rain on his lips. I parted my lips and slipped my tongue inside of his mouth, which was so warm and inviting. His hand tangled itself in my wet hair and pulling me closer to him. Our bodies pressed together, the heat of his chest defying the cold of the rain.

We stood there, kissing in the rain as if it was the most natural thing in the world. Raindrops pounded against the pavement, splattering against windows and shaking the baby leaves on the trees. I was enjoying the taste of rainwater kisses too much to stop.

"We need to get you inside," Owen whispered, pulling himself away. I realized I was shaking like a leaf, my teeth chattering with the cold. He rubbed his hands up and down on my arms, trying to get some warmth back into them before grabbing my hand and pulling me toward the hotel.

It was only a short walk, and we reached the lobby right as another boom of thunder shook the city. I caught my reflection in the elevator door as Owen whisked me up to our room. My lips were blue and my hair was wet, but thankfully my waterproof mascara was holding. My dress was quickly becoming transparent, the water soaking through the white fabric and making it stick to my legs. Luckily, Owen's jacket kept most of me covered, but the dress made me look like I was turning into something that belonged in the water. I gave my reflection a smile, pleased to find I looked more like a sea-soaked mermaid than a drowned rat.

Owen opened the door, and we stepped inside. The balcony doors had been thrown open by the wind, the curtains billowing in gusts. Owen went to close them, but I caught his arm. I didn't want to wait a second longer to have him. His white dress shirt was plastered against his skin, the water making it almost translucent. I could see the gentle slopes and lines of his muscles highlighted by the wet cloth, everything in perfect proportion.

"Leave it open," I whispered, dropping the jacket off my shoulders and reaching to him for a kiss. He wrapped his arms around me, the wet fabric of his shirt cold at first, but heating quickly as his body flared with desire.

I fumbled with the buttons on his shirt, the cold making my fingers clumsy. He growled and ripped it apart, sending buttons flying through the air. Owen stripped the wet dress shirt from his skin, every inch of his toned chest and arms glistening with the dampness. I licked my lip, biting the bottom one and reaching for him again. His skin was cold, in perfect contrast with the fire that burned inside of me.

The doors banged against their hinges as a cold spray from the storm blew in, but I didn't care. How could I care with a man as attractive as Owen standing half-naked in front of me. His eyes met mine, dark and hungry, a need filling them to the point of pain. He pressed his mouth against mine, his lips cool but his tongue hot. The contrast was startling and wonderful, making me ache to take him completely inside me.

I nibbled my way along his jawline, feeling his shoulders flex beneath my fingers, a small moan of want escaping his perfect lips. I kissed his Adam's apple, down the the strong curve of his collarbone, down to one hard, erect nipple. He groaned slightly, tangling his fingers in my hair as I took it in my mouth. It was rock solid from the cold, and I could only imagine the pleasure my hot mouth was sending through him as I flicked it with my tongue.

Slowly, I worked my way lower, kneeling in front of the bulge growing in his pants. With a wicked grin, I looked up and worked the zipper down on his dress pants. As the button came loose in my hands, his manhood stood ready for me. Inching the wet pants off his sculpted ass, followed quickly by his boxers and socks, I soon had him completely naked in front of me.

I stared at his perfection. The rain gleamed on his muscles, tiny drops of water that I envied for being able to touch him so closely.

"Kaylee..." I loved the way my name sounded on his lips, his voice thrillingly gruff. I looked up at him through my eyelashes, watching his face react to sheer pleasure as I took him into my mouth. He groaned with satisfaction, his eyes closing and his fingers grabbing at my hair. I rocked gently back and forth, sucking and licking, enjoying the taste of his skin. He seemed to grow in my mouth, swelling with a need only I could meet.

He pulled up gently on my hair as I stopped to take a breath, coaxing me to my feet. He gave me an appreciative smile before a concerned look took over his face.

"Kaylee, you're shivering." He ran his hands up and down along my bare skin, goosebumps covering every inch. I wasn't sure if I was shivering from the cold, or from pure desire making me vibrate with need.

"We need to warm you up," he said softly, an eager grin spreading across his face. "Let's get you out of those wet clothes."

Strong fingers slid the straps of my soaked dress from my shoulders, a sheen of wetness coating my entire body. Slowly, so slowly I almost begged him to go quicker so I could touch him again, he peeled my dress from my body, followed by the sheer panties. Inch by inch he worked the wet fabric down, caressing every part of my skin until I was bare and trembling before him. With every stroke, warm tendrils of sensation swirled across my chilled skin.

My teeth started chattering, despite my best efforts to stop them. My desire was red hot, but my body was chilled to the bone. Owen effortlessly swept me into his arms, and in three steps we were in the marble bathroom, the usually cold tile feeling warm against my frozen feet as Owen gently set me down.

He stepped into the giant glass shower, his ass just begging to be spanked. I reached out to touch it, giving the firm muscle a good squeeze. He tightened, showing off the full strength of his ass. A thrill of anticipation surged through me. The water hissed as Owen stepped back out, letting the shower get to full heat. In one smooth motion, he closed the bathroom door and pulled me close to him. Steam was already beginning to condense on the mirror, the room growing warm.

"Now, where were we?" he whispered into my ear, his hand tracing the line of my shoulder. I kissed him, showing him exactly where we had left off. He kissed me again, a no-holds-barred kiss that rocked my world. My body shifted from rainwater ice to shower steam hot, the fire within me begging to be quenched by him.

He continued trailing down my arm, his fingers tracing the hollow of my elbow before making the leap to my ribs. With eyes intent on mine, he cupped my breast in his hand, strumming the erect nipple with his thumb. Desire thrummed through me, vibrating my body as though I were a guitar string. He kissed me again, sending me straight to heaven as he played my body like a musical instrument.

"Owen...please, I need you," I gasped. I ached in only a way he could soothe.

With a low animal growl he picked me up and placed me on the edge of the sink. The room was thick with steam, the white mist swirling around the room and fogging the mirror. Owen stood before me, his manhood ready to take me. I guided him in, gasping at the wonderful sensation as he filled me to breaking. My legs wrapped around him, pulling him deeper and deeper into me.

I dug my nails into his back as he thrust, his ass flexing and releasing against my calf muscles. My moans echoed through the marble bathroom, begging him for more. A sheen of sweat broke out across his brow as his muscles worked.

He grabbed my hips and pulled me off the sink, flipping me around. My hands went to the mirror to steady myself as he pulled my hips back toward him. He was within me again in a moment, his face reflecting pure lust in the fogged mirror. His hands went to the mirror as he pressed his body against mine, pushing and pulling, the two of us working in tandem to create pure bliss.

Owen's speed increased, his hips bucking back and forth, putting his hands on my hips to guide me where he wanted. The heat of his hands, the motion of his hips, the breathless groans of delight were sending me toward climax. I could tell he was climbing with me, the two of us crashing into sweet oblivion at the same time.

His thrusting slowed, and my body trembled from pleasure rather than cold. I felt like I might never stop shaking and I was all right with that. Owen turned me toward him, wrapping his arms around me and kissing me deeply.

"You're still too cold," he said with a grin, gently pushing me toward the steaming glass shower. I stepped inside, letting the hot water sluice down my body. My feet burned a little as the lingering cold finally escaped my flesh. Owen closed the glass door behind him, looking me up and down with obvious approval.

"What?" I asked, catching the hot water in my hands and pouring it over my shoulders.

"You are just so damn beautiful," he said softly, the word beautiful echoing off the glass walls. "Turn around."

I turned so I was facing the shower head, a blush heating my face from the compliment. When Owen said I was beautiful, I believed him.

Owen placed one hand on my bicep, wrapping the other around to my front. I moaned softly as he explored my feminine folds, questing for my pleasure center. He found it quickly, letting out a raw sound of male appreciation at my wetness. Using soft circles, he began to massage and tease, coaxing me toward bliss. I leaned back into him, letting myself get lost in the moment.

"You are so incredibly sexy," he whispered, his lips brushing against my shoulder and adding to the fabulous sensations coursing through my body. "You turn me on so much. I love the way you taste."

My body started to tremble, his words and fingers sending me to the point of no return. He kept whispering in my ear, "You feel so tight and amazing. You feel so good. Come for me, Kaylee."

With a cry, my body shuddered, the lights swirling into a kaleidoscope of color and pleasure. My knees buckled, unable to support the sheer volume of bliss coursing through me. Owen held me up, his fingers still working their magic, making my body vibrate with bliss.

When he finally released me, my breaths came in ragged pants. His arms stayed strong around me, holding me so I wouldn't fall to my knees in happy surrender. He kissed my shoulder, sending a shiver down my spine. I turned slowly to find him breathing almost as hard as I was.

The lights suddenly flickered as thunder boomed, shaking the windows outside. Owen and I exchanged a quick glance before promptly exiting the shower. I glanced at the mirror and started laughing, Owen joining in as he followed my gaze.

The mirror was littered with hand-prints. It was incredibly obvious exactly what we had been doing, the perfect mirror smudged with our escapades. Owen let out a hearty chuckle, pulling me into him for yet another mind-blowing kiss.

"Be right back," he finally whispered, letting me go. I stood there for a moment, dizzy from his kiss. Thunder boomed again, but the lights stayed bright. I had completely forgotten about the balcony doors until I heard Owen closing them. I smiled as I wrapped myself up in a towel, knowing he was making sure the room was warm for me.

Owen opened the door, the steam leaking out into the main room as he stepped inside wearing one of the hotel's voluminous robes. He handed me a second, the material soft and luxurious. I followed him out. The room dark. He hopped on the bed and motioned me to follow.

Lightning illuminated the sky through the windows. Owen had drawn the drapes back so we could watch the night sky light up. I cuddled into the nook of his shoulder, a delightful warm drowsy feeling washing over me. The sky lit up as thunder echoed through the city buildings, shaking windows and rattling doors. I wasn't scared, though. With Owen holding me, the world could end, and I would still be safe.

CHAPTER SEVENTEEN

The plane touched down and woke me from the blurry vestiges of a strange dream. As I opened my eyes sleepily, I saw Owen's smiling face. It had been a rough flight. The first four hours, Owen had managed to keep me relatively calm and distracted, but when we hit a patch of turbulence, I had lost it. Luckily, Owen had convinced me to take some medication to help me relax, and then had held me until I fell asleep. I was safe in his arms, and I managed to sleep through the rest of the flight, albeit with very strange dreams. Presently, the medication was still in my system, but at least this time I was going to get off the airplane and not have a wicked hangover.

"Good morning, gorgeous. Welcome to Dubai." He kissed me gently and pushed open one of the window shades. Bright white sunshine poured into the dimly lit cabin, making me blink. I fumbled in my bag for a brush, ran it through my hair, then quickly gathered my things to get off the plane.

As the door opened, I felt a blast of heat, like I had just stepped into an oven. Nothing could have prepared me for how hot it was. Not even when I had gone to the Caribbean had I ever been this hot. There was no moisture in the air here, no clouds. *No wonder it was a desert,* I thought. I was used to summers in Iowa, where the humidity and the heat make the corn grow sweet, but this was a different kind of heat. Sand and blue skies were all I could see, and everything seemed to be reflecting the gleaming sunlight back upon itself.

The airport where we had landed was small and obviously for wealthy clients with private jets. I felt like a movie star as I walked down the stairs and onto a red carpeted walkway.

A private car was waiting to take us to our hotel. I wondered what a city would look like in this part of the world. As someone who never expected to travel, and never had the desire to either, I hadn't paid much attention to the places I could go. Even when Owen had told me where we were going, my knowledge was limited and scattered.

I had began to watch a brief "Cultural Awareness" video while we were on the airplane, but I hadn't lasted long. All I knew about Dubai was that it was known for its oil and that the world's tallest building, the Burj Khalifa, was located there.

I looked out the window as the city came into

view and gasped. It was quite possibly the most unique city I could have imagined. The pictures online didn't do it justice. Skyscrapers soared into the atmosphere, their shapes almost whimsical. I could see part of the Burj Khalifa as we drove closer, its spire threading into the sky past where I could follow it. The thought of going to the top made my stomach feel a little queasy.

The car drove us through the city, whose buildings were all beautiful and unique. I had expected it to look like New York City, or maybe Chicago, but this was beyond anything I could have imagined. I smiled as I gazed at the structure. I didn't know that it was possible to make skyscrapers that looked like sailboats.

The car slowly worked it's way toward the base of the *massive* tower of the Burj Khalifa. At 2,722 feet and 162 floors: it dominated the skyline. My neck ached as I craned it backward to see the top, but we were too close and the tower was too tall. The car dropped us off, and Owen and I headed inside the main lobby.

Everything inside was sleek and modern, made for a worldwide stage. Businessmen in western attire mingled with men wearing the traditional long white *dishdasha*. A woman in a *hijab* stood next to a Russian woman in jeans and a tank-top, both of them waiting for their husbands. I tried my best not to stare at the non-Western clothing, but it was just something that I had never seen before. It was exotic and very, very foreign.

Owen didn't stop to check in at the desk, he just

headed straight for the elevators. The shiny doors closed and shot us up fast enough to make my ears pop. Owen led me confidently out of the elevator and down a hallway, apparently very used to the layout of the place as he spent so much time here for his business trips,. A man was waiting for us outside of a dark wooden door. I smiled as I recognized who it was. At least not everything was foreign here.

Dean grinned as soon as he saw us, quickly sliding a keycard into the door and opening it. As I walked past, he touched my shoulder and whispered, "I'm glad you made it." I couldn't help but flash him a grin, glad to have another familiar face in a sea of new ones.

"How did you get here? Aren't you supposed to be watching Emma?" I asked him.

Dean shrugged. "She asked if I could switch with Mr. Parker's usual bodyguard for the trip. Mr. Saunders was all too happy to agree. Besides," he said with a quick grin. "I thought you could use the friendly face."

"You know me too well," I said softly as I stepped through the door. I sent Emma a silent thank you. Knowing I had Dean looking out for me, someone I already trusted, made the idea of being somewhere so foreign easier.

Owen sat down on a white, beautifully upholstered sofa, kicking his shoes off and relaxing for a moment. He watched me as I explored the room like a little kid, grinning at my shock at the size and lavishness of it all. There was a study with a giant TV, a huge and inviting bedroom with a massive bathroom, and a living room bigger than my apartment. The bar and pantry were better stocked than my own, but I forgot it all when I saw the view. From the windows, I could see the city, the desert, and even a sliver of the Gulf glimmering in the distance. It was absolutely breathtaking.

"What do you think?" Owen asked with a grin as I found my way back to the living room. He lounged comfortably on the couch as though he had always lived there. Unable to find the words I needed, my mouth opened and closed like a fish.

"This room is nicer than my parents' house. I can't wrap my head around how big this place is. I didn't know this level of niceness even existed. I don't think this even qualifies as a hotel anymore. I'm in awe."

Owen laughed and stood. He walked over to me and kissed me affectionately on the nose.

"I'm glad you like it. Make yourself comfortable." He began to throw on his suit jacket again. "I need to get some work done in the office, but come in if you need anything. I'd suggest something simple for dinner tonight, but we already have plans. I know you must be jet-lagged, but I need you to be ready to go to the sheik's palace tonight for dinner. I'm sorry."

I nodded, accepting the apology, and Owen smiled at me. He turned and entered the study, closing the door gently behind him. In my mind's eye, I could see him opening his laptop and setting up his phone, placing everything he needed just so on the desk before getting to work. It made me smile as I headed toward the bedroom to unpack and settle in.

***

Rachel and Emma had done well at their job of picking out my clothes. Owen's eyes practically popped out of his head when he saw me in the formal dinner dress they had chosen. It was a deep hue of blue that reminded me of twilight, right as stars start to appear but before the moon rises. The sweetheart cut would have been out of place for a conservative dinner, but with a skin-tight long-sleeve lace overlay the length of the dress, only discrete windows of my skin were exposed. I felt like something out of a fashion magazine. As we walked into the sheik's mansion, I knew that that was the point. I was here as Owen's arm candy tonight.

Sheik Mohammad al-Saffar greeted us warmly as we entered a large open room in the center of what I could only call a palace. Marble archways and lavish gardens made his home exactly what I had imagined the castle from Aladdin to look like in real life.

The older gentleman wore the traditional white dishdasha that I was already associating with the Middle East. He looked exactly like what I thought a sheik would look like. "Mr. Parker, what a pleasure," the sheik greeted Owen with perfect, though slightly accented, English. I wasn't quite sure what I had been expecting, but it wasn't that.

Owen had warned me that as a woman, and not party to the negotiations going on through DS Oil and Gas, I would largely be ignored. I chose not to be slighted as the sheik only nodded, but never spoke to me. As the two men conversed, I followed them into a large dining area. A table big enough to feed a small city dominated the center of the room, and delicious smells were wafting off of covered plates waiting to be devoured.

As the three of us entered the airy room, a young man stood and gracefully padded over to greet us. He wore a western outfit of gray slacks and a white short-sleeved shirt with a collar. He couldn't have been more than a year or two older than I was, with perfect olive skin, dark eyes, and eyelashes that seemed to go on into infinity. He broke into a bright smile as he held out his hand to greet us.

"This is my son, Rashid." The sheik introduced the young man, a proud smile lighting his creased face. It was easy to see that Rashid was his father's pride and joy. Owen shook the younger man's hand, and then followed the father toward the dinner table.

"Please, call me Roger. It's so much easier that way," the young man said without a trace of his father's accent. He reached out his hand to shake mine. I took his hand, surprised at the strength and heat in his fingers. He stared into my eyes, making my cheeks flush when he didn't release my hand. The blush only seemed to amuse him, and he gave me a crooked smirk, knowing that he had flustered me.

I withdrew my hand and hurried to the table. I sat down next to Owen, and Roger took his place across the table from me with his father. The two business men jumped into a conversation regarding their oil dealings almost immediately, using the dinner as a sort of informal business meeting. Roger and I sat quietly as they spoke, his eyes catching mine as often as he could. I shifted in my seat. I was unable to put my finger on it, but something about him made me anxious.

Roger grinned at me, making sure he had my attention as he licked his lips suggestively. I felt the blush start again, but I tried to ignore the flustered feeling rising in my stomach.

I was with Owen. I thought it was fairly clear that I was taken, but Roger didn't seem to care, flirting openly with me across the table, even with Owen right there. I didn't want to do anything that could jeopardize Owen's business dealings, and making the sheik's son unhappy would not indenture any good will, so I sat quietly and focused on the food in front of me, avoiding his smiles.

It wasn't hard to concentrate on the food, though as I had never experienced anything quite like this. There were roasted scallops with black truffles, pan-fried sea bass in a zesty lemon caper sauce, freshly sauteed dandelion root with onion salad, and for dessert something called *la sfera.* It was a beautiful creation of vanilla cream, violet crème brulee, and cassis sorbet that resembled an edible Faberge egg.

We ate until I was sure I couldn't eat another

bite. As a waiter quietly picked up the empty dessert trays, Sheik al-Saffar leaned back in his chair, musing over something Owen had said. He and Owen had spent the entire meal debating various points of the contract that Owen was attempting to secure for Jack's company. This dinner was never meant for me, so I didn't mind the two of them talking shop the entire time. From what little I could understand of their oil jargon, it seemed to be going well.

I was slightly unnerved, however, by Roger's constant attention. He hadn't said a word over dinner, but his eyes had never left me. I felt like he wanted to have me for dinner instead of the sea bass, and he was just waiting to find the opportune moment to catch me. I shivered slightly, but not from cold.

The sheik and Owen stood as soon as the last plates were cleared away, and they walked somewhat sedately toward an attached room with a large TV screen. They wanted to look at one of the advertising campaigns Owen had created for selling al-Saffar's oil to new markets. I smiled for a moment as I knew that meant Owen's task was going well, but then frowned as I realized it meant that Roger and I were left alone at the table.

"Have you ever been to Paris?" Roger asked, playing with a water glass. There was something to the motion that made me uncomfortable. I pushed aside my feelings of discomfort, determined to do my best to help Owen out. If I was going to be traveling with him, I would have to get good at being a well-behaved guest.

"No. This is actually the first time I've been out of the country. Well, other than to the Caribbean, but that almost doesn't count." I gave him my most diplomatic smile and hoped he wouldn't see right through it. I didn't really want to talk to him.

"Would you like to?" He dipped his finger into the glass.

"Um, maybe someday. I've never really had the opportunity to travel, so I've never really thought about it." I gave myself a mental pat on the back for the smooth answer.

"I meant, would you like to go there with me?" He raised his wet finger to his lips, sucking the moisture from his fingertip. I swallowed hard.

"As long as Owen gets to come too," I answered. I hoped that reminding him that I was here with Owen would make him back off. I didn't like how this conversation was going.

"I was thinking just the two of us. It is the city of love, after all." He smiled suggestively at me. I opened my mouth, but no words came out. My brain was scrambling for a diplomatic answer, one that wouldn't make the situation more awkward. Something that would help Owen land this contract.

He laughed, delighting in my discomfort. I played with my water glass, biting the inside of my cheek. If I had been back home I would have told him off. I would have walked out or found someone else to talk to, but I couldn't here. I had to be polite and not do those things for Owen's sake. I couldn't let him down.

"That's a kind offer, but I'm afraid I'm not interested." I finally managed to get out the words, even punctuating them with a smile. His eyes narrowed on me and I felt like a bug caught under a magnifying glass.

"What would you like to do tomorrow, then?"

Nothing with you, I wanted to scream. I glanced over to where I had seen Owen last, glad to see him heading back my direction.

"I'm afraid I have a very busy schedule." That sounded diplomatic enough to me.

"You and I are going to see each other. I'll see to it. I think we could do some amazing things together." The way he said it almost sounded like a threat.

"You'll have to clear that with Owen. He is the one in charge of where I go and who I see." Owen and the sheik paused in a doorway, talking like old friends. I hoped Owen would come back to the table soon. This conversation was making me very uncomfortable, and I wanted it to stop. I didn't want to be diplomatic to Roger anymore.

"That won't be a problem. He and my father have business meetings all day tomorrow. It can be just the two of us." I was an ant again under his magnifying glass.

"I'll still have to clear it with him. Thank you again for the offer," I said hastily, standing up and stepping away before he could say any more. The last thing in the world I wanted to do was see him tomorrow. If I had my way, I would have set him down hard, told him in no uncertain terms that I wasn't interested, but I needed to be tactful for Owen's sake. His contract negotiations hinged on the sheik's favor, and thus, the sheik's son's favor as well.

Owen's brows tightened for a moment as I walked over to him, but he quickly relaxed his face before the sheik could see it. He put his hand on my back, his touch feather light but sending a bolt of security through me. I was safe with Owen. I could see Roger still lounging at the table, a frightening grin on his face. He knew I had fled because of him, and he liked it.

"Thank you for the wonderful dinner. I will make the adjustments you suggested and get back to you in the morning." Owen gave the sheik a perfect businessman smile. I liked the one he gave me better, but I knew the effect that smile could have on people.

The sheik barely batted an eyelash as he reminded Owen of a key point he wanted changed. No wonder the man was worth a fortune if he could evade Owen's charms. The two of them shook hands one final time, and Owen guided me out toward a waiting car. The night air was cooler than I had expected, but the shiver that went through me wasn't from the breeze. It was from Roger's eyes following me out the door.

CHAPTER EIGHTEEN

"I'll be back in time for us to go get something for dinner tonight. Are you sure you'll be all right staying in the hotel today? I can get someone to show you around the city or something." Owen frowned slightly as I adjusted his tie. I made sure it laid straight and then smoothed the fabric across his shoulders. I loved these simple moments. They may never make a scrapbook, but that will stay in my mind forever as perfect.

"I'll be fine. I think I'm still a little jet-lagged, so staying in sounds nice today. Maybe I'll go down to the spa or something later," I said, smiling up at him. His blue eyes still held a pout, so I added, "Besides, Dean will be here with me today if I change my mind."

Owen glanced over to the kitchen where Dean

sat reading a newspaper. He sighed and looked down at me. "You're sure you don't want to do anything today?"

"Yes! Now get going, or you'll be late!" I said, pushing him toward the door. The worry vanished from his eyes as he picked up his briefcase and reached for the doorknob.

"I love you, Kaylee," said Owen, catching my eyes with his. I could feel a happy warmth surge across the connection, filling me with an inner light.

"I love you, Owen. Now, get to work!" I gave him a light peck on the cheek and he grinned before disappearing out the door. The door clicked shut, and I leaned my back against it. I closed my eyes and counted the hours until he would be home, finding them far too many. I hoped that Rashid wouldn't follow through on his threat to come by. I didn't say anything about it to Owen. I didn't want him to worry. Besides, it was probably just an empty threat anyway.

When I opened my eyes again, Dean was standing in front of me.

"Why don't you want to go anywhere today?" he asked softly, his light blue eyes intense as he read the worry on my face. I sighed.

"Rashid, the sheik's son. He makes me uncomfortable, and last night, he said we were going to do something tomorrow. If I stay in the hotel, then I'm hoping he won't bother me."

Dean nodded. "You know I won't let him do anything, right?"

I smiled. Dean, while tall and in amazing shape,

appeared lanky and unimposing. I'm sure he could hold his own in a fight, but he didn't look that scary to me. I wondered how he had gotten the job of guarding billionaires, but I always figured he just had other talents that made him a good bodyguard. I knew he was smart, and if he was good at preventing a bad situation, then that was always better than being scary enough to stop one.

"Thanks, Dean. I know I shouldn't let him get to me, but just something about him set my teeth on edge." I shivered at the memory of him looking at me.

"I've learned to trust those gut instincts. I'll make sure he doesn't bother you today."

"Dean, what about tomorrow though? He's the sheik's son. If things keep going as well as they have between Owen and the sheik, I'm going to have to see him again. There is already another dinner scheduled for tomorrow night." I leaned back against the door again, my shoulders slumping.

"Has he done anything to actually make you concerned?" Dean's eyes narrowed as he contemplated my options.

"No. Just implied. I have no real reason to be afraid of him. He just makes me nervous is all. If I can avoid him, I want to."

Dean nodded, then gave me a warm smile. "Well, don't you worry about him. He's probably just a weird kid who never learned to be polite because he has so much money he never had to. Let Owen know, though. Owen won't stop scheduling things that involve Rashid if you don't tell him.

He'll understand."

I fiddled with the groove in the tile of the entryway, pushing the hem of my yoga pants into it with my toes. "I'll tell him. I just don't want him to be upset or do something that will endanger his contract. It's pretty obvious the sheik thinks his little boy is the best thing since sliced bread and will take any affront to Rashid as an affront to him. I don't want to ruin the contract because some punk makes me nervous."

Dean put his hands on my shoulders, and said in a low voice, "Owen knows how to handle situations like the one with Rashid and his father. You have to trust Owen to do the right thing."

I nodded. "I'll tell him when he gets home. I just feel like I'm overreacting, and I don't want to mess things up."

Dean gave me a squeeze before letting go of my shoulders. His quiet confidence and the way he approached a problem reminded me a lot of my dad. I could see why Emma trusted him as much as she did.

"So, what are you going to do today?" Dean asked, taking a step back into the main room. I glanced about, and my eyes settled on the kitchen. I loved cooking, and I hadn't had time to cook anything more than a frozen pizza for weeks. I had been itching to try out some new recipes after all the good food I had been eating.

"You like pancakes?"

Dean nodded and rubbed his stomach. "Can't you tell?"

"Then get ready for the best pancakes you've ever had. I'm cooking today."

***

"You have the list?"

Dean gave me a look that very clearly said *Of course I have the list. Stop asking.*

I went through the recipes one more time, making sure I had everything. I only wanted Dean to go out shopping for me once. He said he was happy to go do it, that he even knew of a market close by, but I still felt bad. I didn't want to leave the hotel, so I was just going to stay in the room. Dean was all right with that, because I couldn't possibly get into trouble. Besides, if anything did happen, hotel security was on speed dial.

"Remember, fresh cilantro if they have it," I reminded him one last time as he slid on a baseball cap.

"I'll remember. I be back in thirty minutes," Dean said, closing the door behind him. The lock clicked loudly in the quiet room.

I stood staring at the door for a moment, wondering what I should do until he got back. While playing checkers with Dean all day, we had started talking about food. When our favorite homemade meals had come up, I had told him about my mom's secret recipe for "Cheeseburger Pie. Dean suggested I cook it for Owen, along with some chocolate chip cookies. It wasn't exactly scallops with black truffles, but I thought Owen would enjoy it and it gave me something to do. The hotel-stocked kitchen had most of the main ingredients, but I needed some fresh things that I couldn't substitute. For a small slice of my infamous Cheeseburger Pie, Dean had agreed to get them.

I went to the kitchen, pulling out the various pots and pans I would need for cooking and prepping what I could without my fresh ingredients. I found myself humming as I put water on to boil for the potatoes and set out the cutting boards to prep the salad. I was looking for a second mixing bowl when I heard a noise in the other room. Dean was faster than I thought.

I peeked around the corner to the living room, and my blood ran cold. Rashid was on the couch, sitting there like he owned the place. I nearly threw the wooden spoon in my hand at his head, but decided that probably wouldn't be the best reaction. A fair reaction, but not the best.

"How did you get in here, Rashid?" I hoped my annoyance was apparent. I didn't want him here, and I wasn't going to be polite after he broke into my room. I could be diplomatic, but that didn't mean I had to be nice.

He gave me a chastising look. "It's Roger." Then shrugged his shoulders as if getting into a locked hotel room were nothing. "I believe the expression is 'I know a guy.' I get whatever I want, and I wanted to come see you."

I swallowed hard, glancing at the clock. Dean wouldn't be back for another fifteen minutes at the earliest. I hoped there wasn't traffic or that he didn't take his time looking for fresh cilantro. Roger stretched out on the couch, then patted the seat next to him. I stayed standing.

"What do you want to do today, Kaylee?" He looked me up and down, undressing me with his eyes. I fought the urge to cover myself with my hands. He couldn't see through my shirt and yoga pants, no matter how much he wanted to.

"I want you to leave."

"Aw, Kaylee. I can't do that. I came all this way just to see you. Don't be a bad hostess," he said as he stood. I was suddenly very aware of just how much taller he was than I.

"Please leave." I tried to say it forcefully, but it just came out as a whisper. I didn't want to mess anything up for Owen's contract with Roger's father, but I desperately wanted him to go away. He just smirked at me, knowing exactly the position I was in. He knew I wouldn't do anything to jeopardize the contract and he was counting on it. He took a step closer to me.

"You don't want that, baby. You know you want me." His voice was smooth like oil, sliding over my skin and making me feel dirty. I bumped into the wall behind me, not even aware that I had been stepping back. He gave me a smug smile, knowing I had backed myself into a corner.

I spied the phone on a small table. With my left hand, I reached for the phone's receiver, but my right hand never got to the numbered buttons. As fast as a snake, he grabbed my hand. The receiver fell out of my hand, and I looked up at him with fear in my eyes. I struggled, but his hands were bigger and stronger than mine, and held me easily. I tried to bring my knee up into his groin or at least to drag my foot down his shin- anything to cause him pain- but he was pressed so close to me I couldn't move. I was powerless to stop him, no matter how much I fought and squirmed.

His cologne filled my nostrils. It was strong, like he had bathed in the bottle instead of a shower, and sickeningly sweet. I wanted to throw up. I wanted to be anywhere but here, with anyone but him.

"Please, don't," I whispered, struggling against him. He just laughed, the sound striking fear deep into my bones. Where was Dean?

"Just relax, Kaylee. You'll enjoy this so much more if you just relax," he said softly, his breath giving me unpleasant chills. The calmness and surety in the way he moved told me this wasn't the first time he had done this.

"Get away from her." A commanding voice boomed from across the room. I felt my knees go weak with relief as the door slammed behind Dean. Roger turned his head to glance at him, but didn't let me go.

"This isn't your problem, man. Beat it." Roger turned back, leering at me. He wasn't afraid of Dean.

Before I could move, Roger was ripped off of me like an old band-aid and thrown to the ground. He lay on his back, a dazed expression on his face as Dean stood over him like a tiger about to pounce.

With a shake of his head, Roger rolled to his

side, then up to his feet. Dean moved around to stand between me and Roger, gliding along the floor like a big cat. I rubbed my wrists, trying to keep my panic under control.

"Get out." Dean's voice was like ice.

"She wanted it, man," Roger said, trying to appeal to Dean. "Just wait until my father hears about this." Dean's face only hardened. Roger swallowed and started backing up toward the exit. He stopped and gave me a wink and an evil smile. "I *own* this city. There isn't anywhere you can go to escape me, so I'll see you later, Kaylee."

I shuddered, then looked back at Dean. When I first met Dean, I didn't understand how he was a bodyguard to the billionaires. He was tall and in shape, but he just wasn't physically imposing. Now, watching as he strode toward Rashid, his eyes gleaming violence, I understood. I would willingly take on ten muscle-men bodybuilders before I even thought about messing with Dean.

In one fluid motion, Dean had Roger pressed against the wall, his hands wrapped in the front of Roger's shirt. Roger started spluttering, the whites of his eyes growing bigger until he looked like a scared rabbit. Dean held him there, then leaned in and whispered something. I couldn't hear it, but somehow Roger's eyes grew even bigger. His hand started scratching at the wall, desperately looking for the door handle to make his escape.

Dean let him go, pushing off of him like he didn't want the stench of Roger on his hands. Roger scrambled for the door, running like a beaten dog with his tail between his legs. The door slammed shut behind him as he scampered down the hallway.

"Are you okay?" Dean asked, turning to me. He grabbed my wrists and looked them over, checking for any sign of damage. A single tear rolled down my cheek.

"He was gonna... he was gonna.." I couldn't get the words out. They were too horrific. Dean wrapped me up in his arms, protecting me from the world. He touched my hair softly and made a soft soothing *shush* noise as I broke down in tears.

I sank to the floor, and Dean followed me, still holding me. I cried into his shoulder, letting the terror and frustration work itself out. He just kept quietly comforting me, keeping me safe until I was ready to talk. Finally, the tears wouldn't come anymore and my ragged sobs slowed to where I could speak.

"Are you okay?" Dean asked again, concern showing in every word. I nodded.

"How did he get in here, Dean? I didn't let him in. I was in the kitchen, and then he was just there."

"I don't know, but I'll find out. I'm sure he just bribed someone or stole a key from housekeeping. I'm so sorry, Kaylee. This never should have happened."

I looked up at him, not wanting him to feel guilty for this. This was Roger's fault and no one else's. "There is no way you could have known he was going to do this. I should have been safe here."

Dean sighed and pulled me closer. I liked how secure he made me feel, like the way I did when my dad would keep me safe from monsters. "I still feel bad. It's my job to keep you safe."

"You did. You saved me."

Dean gave me another squeeze, my body still shaking from fear and adrenaline. I felt like I would never stop shaking.

"How did you get here in time? I thought you were still going to be gone for a while," I asked glancing at the clock. My water in the kitchen was boiling. I should turn it off before all the water evaporated.

"There was a sandstorm coming, so I hurried back. I'm afraid I didn't get your cilantro."

I felt a smile crack my face. The cilantro didn't seem so important anymore.

My phone chirped across the room, a text coming in from Owen. Dean and I both looked at it, knowing that we were going to have to tell him. Neither of us moved. If I didn't tell him, maybe I could convince myself it didn't happen. If Owen didn't know, then it was all just a bad dream.

My phone chirped again and Dean released me, standing up and retrieving my phone. I clicked on the message, not quite brave enough yet to call him.

We've been invited to go deep sea fishing on Rashid's yacht. If things kept going this way, Roger and his father would be permanent fixtures in our lives.

My phone slipped from my fingers and clattered to the floor. I didn't even bother picking it up. In my head I could see exactly what was going to happen. The sheik was going to ask Owen for a last minute business meeting, and I would be on the boat alone with Roger. He would come at me again, and this time, there would be no Dean or Owen to save me. I started to cry again at the memory of him touching me, the smell of his cologne, the sick feeling in the pit of my stomach.

Dean's arms were around me again in an instant as I crumpled back to the floor. "I can't do this..." I whispered, my lungs too compressed to get much more than a wheeze out. A cold panic sunk into my bones, every muscle in my body trying to "fight and flight" at the same time. Outside, the sandstorm hit, the wind howling with anger at being denied entrance.

"He's going to be everywhere, Dean. He will never leave me alone. Especially not after today." The fact was like an ice cube in my mind, always bobbing to the top and making everything cold. "He really does own the city, Dean. He and his father have connections to everything. I can't stay here; I'm not safe here anymore. I just want to go home."

Dean pulled out his phone, hitting a speed dial number and waiting patiently until a voice answered on the other end. It was Owen. Just hearing his voice on the other end of the phone sent elation and fear through me.

"Sir, there's been an incident." Dean was the perfect professional.

"What happened? Is Kaylee alright?" The phone wasn't on speaker, but I could still hear his voice clearly. I wished so much that I could bury myself into Owen's chest, let his arms wrap around me, and let this bad memory drift away. I wished I could have made the past thirty minutes different. I felt horrible that this incident would probably sour his relationship with the sheik. I wished I had another option, one that wouldn't have the possibility of destroying what he was working so hard on. I knew I shouldn't be the one feeling guilty, but I couldn't help it. Yet another wave of anger washed through me that Roger would completely and utterly betray my trust and personal space.

"Kaylee is fine, sir. A little shaken, though. I got here just in time." Dean glanced at me. I was still shaking like a leaf in an autumn breeze. He gave my shoulder a slight squeeze, then stood and headed toward the kitchen to tell Owen what had happened. I was grateful that he was giving me space so I didn't have to hear the words happen again.

I looked out at the sand beating against the window. It was beautiful in a way, but I knew I could never survive out there. Lightning flashed amid the swirling brown clouds. There was no moisture out there, only swirling, hateful sand. It was as if Mother Nature herself was telling me that I didn't belong in this place.

"Yes, sir, I understand. I'll see to it. Thank you, sir." Dean came over and handed me the phone. My hands were shaking so badly that I almost dropped it.

"Owen?" I was surprised that my voice didn't come out as a squeak. It sounded normal.

"Are you alright, Kaylee? I'll come home right now, sandstorm be damned." He sounded angry, but

I knew his anger wasn't directed at me though.

"I'm okay. A little shaky, but I'm okay. Really." If I told him I was okay and he believed it, then maybe I really would be. "Please wait until the storm is over. Dean is with me and I don't need you getting turned into a sand zombie."

"Kaylee, I want you to know that I'm not going to let this kind of behavior slide." Owen's voice vibrated with a quiet rage. I was very glad he was on my side.

"Thank you, Owen," I said softly.

"I'll call back in a little bit, okay?"

I nodded, not caring that he couldn't see me as the line went quiet. I let the phone fall to my lap as I just stared out at the raging storm that would never yield any rain.

***

When the storm finally ended, the world returned to too-bright sunshine and blue skies. Down below, I could see workers with brooms pushing piles of sand from the sidewalks, the clean-up already beginning. Owen was home shortly, almost as soon as the sky was clear.

"Kaylee," he called, barging into the room. I got up from the couch, knowing I was pale and trembling. I was in his arms before I could take a second breath.

Owen held me tight against his chest, his heart pounding wildly. I held onto him like he was the only solid thing in my world, a strong rock to hold onto among the swirling sands. He kept his arms around me, but looked down, releasing me slightly to brush a stray strand of hair from my face.

"You're sure you're okay?"

"If either of you asks me that again, I will hit you," I said, glancing toward Dean. He sat protectively by the door, a lion guarding his den. "Look, I made you both some dinner. I don't want to talk about what happened right now. I just want to eat."

The two men shared a glance and nodded. I knew the smells coming from the kitchen were intoxicating. Once I had hung up with Owen, I had dived into my cooking. It was something that required my concentration and allowed me to distance myself from what had just happened. I wasn't ready to deal with it yet.

Owen put on a smile, his face attempting to convince his brain that everything was okay. "What did you make? It smells wonderful."

"Cheeseburger Pie, a salad, and cookies." I motioned them both to the table and brought out a steaming casserole dish.

"What's cheeseburger pie? I don't think I've ever heard of it," Owen said, eying the baking dish in my hands.

"It's basically meatloaf with mashed potatoes and lots and lots of cheese. I had to improvise on the salad a little bit, but I think it came out pretty good. I'll put the cookies in the oven in just a couple minutes so they'll come out warm when we want to eat them." I smiled at the two men.

It was so much easier to just pretend that nothing had happened. I didn't want that afternoon to be real, so I chose not to think about it. I knew that I was going to have to face it eventually, but I didn't want to do it right this minute. I wanted to pretend, just for a little while, that everything was normal and things were going to work out the way they should. I just wanted to forget.

We ate quietly as the sun began to sink and the world turned dark. I put the dishes in the sink and we sat on the couches eating cookies, only making small-talk. When the cookies were gone, Dean volunteered to do dishes. I watched as Owen turned his phone on, which was bizarre because he never had his phone turned off. It immediately chirped at him and he went into the next room to work on it.

I sat on the couch. The room dipped into darkness as night fell across the city. For the first time since I was a small child, the dark made me nervous. I was sure every noise in the hallway was Roger trying to sneak back in. Every creak of the giant building made me feel sure that something terrible was about to happen.

I ran around the room, turning on every light I could find, but it didn't get rid of the fear. Owen came out and sat beside me on the couch, trying his best to be strong and comforting. I knew I was jumping at shadows, but that didn't make me any less stressed out.

A key slid into the door and the handle moved. I froze, but the door didn't unlock. A panic swept through me. I knew it was Roger coming back to take his revenge on the three of us. Would he be armed this time? Owen looked at me, his face going pale. Dean moved to the door like a hunting cat, opening it like he was expecting to jump on his prey.

A very startled businessman looked up at Dean with wide eyes, his hand holding the keycard in midair. "I must have the wrong room! So sorry!" he yelped, quickly scurrying out from under Dean's predatory gaze. Dean watched him disappear down the hall before closing the door.

"I'll be right outside if you need me," he said softly, knowing that Owen and I needed to talk. I waited until the door clicked shut before speaking.

"I can't stay here." I could feel a tear trickling down my cheek. I hated being afraid. "I want to go home."

Owen's brows furrowed. "Are you sure? We could get another hotel?'

"I know he would just find us again. Besides, we're supposed to have dinner with him tomorrow night. His father is the man you are here to see. I'm so sorry, Owen, but I can't stay here."

"Kaylee, I don't know what to do here. I want to do my job, but I want to make sure you are safe. You are more important to me, but I want to make sure that's really what you want."

"I know this contract is important to you Owen. I never meant to make things complicated-"

Owen cut me off before I could finish the sentence. "This is not your fault, Kaylee. Rashid is a jerk and if his father can't see past that to do business then he is an idiot."

I smiled, glad that Owen would be on my side no matter what.

"Owen, this place is your life. Not mine. I don't like it here. The sun, the sand, the foreignness of everything, the constant threat of Roger-- it just makes it clearer and clearer that I don't belong here."

"Maybe next time-" Owen started, but I cut him off this time.

"There will be no next time, Owen. I won't come back here."

Owen went quiet. If I never came back here, then that meant he would spend weeks here alone. We couldn't be together. Thoughts and pain flitted across his face like shadows across the sand dunes.

"I'll take you home, then," he said finally. "We'll leave first thing in the morning."

CHAPTER NINETEEN

"Owen, you don't have to come. You have obligations here," I said softly as we walked in the desert sun to the waiting jet. The red carpet was there once more, along with the stairs into the plane, but I didn't feel glamorous today. I just wanted to go home and forget that this trip ever happened.

"Kaylee, I can't in good conscience let you get on that airplane by yourself. You don't exactly do well on them." He smiled at me, but there was a tension around his eyes which I hadn't seen before. I boarded the airplane first, and I glanced back to see Owen standing at the first step, his gaze at the horizon. He was taking the scenery in as though he might never come back.

I buckled myself into the large leather recliner, settling in and taking some deep, calming breaths.

This airplane wasn't as frightening this time, but I wasn't about to think that I could do this flying thing on a regular basis. Owen sat across from me, looking out the window and resting his hands on his knees. He looked mostly relaxed, save for the tension in his jawline.

I gave him a smile, though in all honesty it was only a curve of my lips since my heart wasn't in it. He mirrored my expression as I popped one of the pills from the previous flight into my mouth. I leaned back, focusing on my breathing and convincing myself that I could do this.

The plane started to rumble forward, the engines turning form a high-pitched whine into a solid roar as the wings met the wind. I could see Owen open up his laptop and begin banging on the keys, a frown across his face. I wondered just how much this little detour was screwing up his business dealings. He was supposed to be meeting with the sheik right now to discuss billions of dollars' worth of contracts, not getting on a plane to fly a terrified girl home.

My ears popped as we rose higher, and I took a deep breath, trying to keep my fear at bay. My body wanted to give into the terror, but I wasn't going to let it. The medication was starting to work itself into my system, making it easier to turn off the instinctual fear.

"Owen?"

He looked up for a moment, annoyed, before smoothing the lines of his face.

"Thank you." I gave him a small smile, hoping

his edginess would subside. He smiled and ran his hand through his golden hair.

"Of course, Kaylee. You know I would do anything for you."

An awkward pause fell between us. I didn't know what to say. How could I thank him for possibly ruining a billion dollar contract because of me? *Because of Roger*, I quickly corrected myself. It wasn't my fault that I no longer felt safe in Dubai. Unfortunately, just because it wasn't my fault, didn't take away the guilty feeling.

There was a space growing between Owen and I that wasn't due to the position of the plane. He was angry about something, the way he banged on his keyboard, and the flash in his eyes giving it away. I knew he wasn't mad at me but rather the situation. I wished for the millionth time that I could change how things had happened. I just wanted to go back to the way things used to be.

"Owen?" I asked, hoping to catch his attention. He made a noncommittal noise, but didn't look up. I didn't continue and instead just leaned my seat back. Something had changed about him, but I couldn't figure out what. The medicine was starting to make me drowsy, and since Owen didn't want to talk, I just let it overpower and carry me off to sleep.

***

Rain beat on the windows of the chauffeured town-car, smearing the lines of Des Moines into sad gray smudges. We drove by Gray's Lake and the crab-apple forest, but the blossoms were long gone. The lake was blocked by cement barriers displaying signs that the park was closed due to flooding. Over the softly playing radio, I could hear a weather report for yet more rain and increasing flooding throughout the area.

Owen and I sat on opposite sides of the vehicle. He hadn't said more than a word since we got off the airplane and into the car. We both knew that something we didn't want was going to happen. The flight had been painfully uncomfortable. Owen had focused on his work as we flew away from the thing he was trying to accomplish, the silence deafening. I appreciated that he was willing to drop everything for me, but I didn't want to ruin his dreams.

It wasn't even so much the leaving that was keeping us quiet; it was the fact that I would never go back. Rashid al-Saffar had too much influence in the region for me to ever feel safe there again. Unfortunately, that was exactly where Owen's job needed him to be. He would travel, and I would have to stay behind. It would be a long distance relationship that would never work. We both knew this was going to be the end, but we were trying to maintain the illusion of us as a couple for as long as possible.

The car pulled to a stop in the parking lot of my building. We sat silently, neither one of us really ready to say goodbye, but knowing it had to be done. The driver exited the car and started moving my suitcases toward my apartment. A small rumble of thunder echoed in the distance, breaking the silence.

"I can't live this lifestyle anymore, Owen. I love you, but I can't do this." The words trickled out with my tears. I didn't want to say them, but they needed to be said.

"There are other places in the world we can go," Owen replied halfheartedly. His dark blue eyes held an ocean of sadness. This wasn't how either of us wanted our relationship to end.

"No, Owen. No matter where we go, I would just end up resenting you, or you resenting me. I let myself get drawn into something I didn't want with my last boyfriend, and it nearly broke me. We have to be equals. We can compromise, but sometimes a person can compromise too much. I love you more than I've ever loved anyone, but I have to stay true to myself. I'm sorry." I felt a hot tear leak out, burning as it slipped down my cheek.

Owen nodded slowly. "I understand." He reached out and wiped the tear from my face with his thumb, cradling my jaw in his hand. His eyes shone with tears as he leaned forward and kissed me softly. I closed my eyes and tried to put every detail of it into my memory. The way his lips were soft against mine, the taste of his skin, the warmth of his hand, the smell of his cologne. I mentally cataloged it, trying to secure it in my mind so I would forever remember it.

"I have to take care of some business, but I promise I'll be back." Owen's hand stayed on my cheek, even as he pulled away. I appreciated the lie. It made leaving the car easier. The driver had returned, shaking raindrops off his hat.

"Goodbye, Owen." I said it so softly I wasn't sure if he heard me. A single tear ran out of the corner of his eye, but he didn't move to brush it away.

"Goodbye, Kaylee," he whispered. I barely heard it as I bolted from the car. Thunder rolled in the distance as the car drove away, but all I could see was the rain.

CHAPTER TWENTY

The next morning I woke to the soft sound of more rain on the roof. I lay in bed, staring at the dark ceiling, trying to fall back asleep but not having any success. My alarm clock told me it was only four in the morning. I groaned and tried to close my eyes one last time, but my body was convinced it was lunchtime and that I needed to get up. I realized that I hated jet lag with a passion.

I got up and walked into the kitchen, ready to start a pot of coffee and get something to eat. Halfway through the living room, I tripped on a laundry basket in the middle of the floor. After shouting swear words at the plastic hamper and threatening to melt it into sporks, I turned on a light and successfully navigated to my coffee pot. As I waited for the coffee to brew, I glanced around the small room. Even in the dim, pre-dawn light, it was a disaster area. *Much like my life*, I thought.

"I'm fixing this," I said aloud to no one. I started by putting the dirty dishes in the dishwasher until the coffee pot sputtered to silence. It felt good to organize and put things away, trying to tame the mess that was my life. Mug in hand, I started to clean up my living room.

Three loads of laundry later, my house was spic-and-span again. I glanced around the room, smiling at how it felt more like home. I glanced at my phone on the now clean coffee table. I hadn't heard it buzz or chirp, and no light was flashing on it to indicate a new message. Before I could stop myself, I picked it up and looked just to make sure I hadn't missed one.

Empty. No new messages. I set it down, wondering if I should send Owen the first message. The blank screen stared up at me. I wasn't sure what part of the world he was in. He never said whether he was going back to Dubai or back to New York. My fingers itched to text him, but I was the one who said I couldn't live his executive lifestyle. I was the one who had asked to go home. I didn't want to get his hopes up for something I couldn't give.

I regarded the silent phone for a moment, willing it to ring. It simply sat there like the piece of plastic it was. I felt like screaming. I needed something to do. If I sat here much longer, I was going to burst into tears and I didn't want to cry anymore. The tears, anger, and hurt were all welling up in my chest, and I wasn't ready to deal with any of it. I wanted the illusion that things were the way they were supposed to be.

I went to the kitchen and started pulling out pots and pans, turning on the oven and pulling out my cookbooks. If I couldn't sit still, at least I could be productive. Flour covered my kitchen in no time as I went to work kneading bread, baking cookies, and using up all the baking supplies in my pantry. I only had a few things in my fridge, so I couldn't do much more than the basics.

After a run of cookies, a loaf of banana bread, and a failed experiment at egg-free brownies, I could go no further with my meager supply of groceries. I knew I wasn't going to eat all the things I had just baked, but at least it was now closer to lunch than to breakfast.

I picked up my phone, fully intent on calling Marissa, and if I happened to check my messages as a result of said phone call, I wasn't going to beat myself up about it. No messages.

I wanted to pout, but instead I did what I had intended, and called Marissa. I knew Allie was working today, but Tuesdays were usually Marissa's day off. All I got was a cheery sounding voice-mail recording.

"Hey, so, I'm back in town. Give me a call when you get this." I tried not to sound as dejected as I felt, but I knew she would see through me in an instant. Getting a call from a friend who is supposed to be on vacation saying they're back in town is a pretty sure way to know something happened.

The urge to do something, anything, was

growing stronger. I needed to get out of the house. There wasn't anything for me here; no reason for me to stay indoors. I hopped in the shower, rinsed the flour out of my hair, and changed into jeans and a comfy shirt. I didn't need to impress anyone today.

A piece of paper fluttered from the door jam as I opened the it. My heart caught for a second as I thought of Owen leaving me a note, but I quickly recognized the apartment building's logo.

Dear Resident,

We are sorry to inform you that the intercom and door lock system for your building is currently broken. Please note that visitors will be able to use the intercom to notify residents of arrival, but the two-way communication and door unlock features are currently unavailable. The resident will have to manually open the door to allow visitors into the building.

We apologize for any inconvenience and hope to have this fixed as soon as possible.

Sincerely,

The Management

I crumpled the paper and tossed it into the trash bin before closing the door. Just my luck that the system would break, I thought. Then, I realized that I didn't have anyone to visit me anymore. My annoyance disappeared into a fog of self-pity as I stepped out to my car.

I headed into downtown Des Moines, looking for something to do. After driving aimlessly through the city, I decided I should at least get groceries. I turned to head toward the highway when I saw the dome for the botanical gardens.

We were in front of the Des Moines Botanical Gardens, the big glass dome glowing slightly from an inner light. Owen stepped out of the car and immediately shrugged out of his jacket and draped it across my shoulders without even asking. It was warm and smelled like his cologne. I took a deep breath, my insides going tingly at being wrapped in the scent. He grabbed my hand in his, his body heat seeping into my palm, and pulled me inside.

The memory hit me, and I turned into the parking lot unsure of what I was expecting to accomplish. Owen wouldn't be here with me this time. But I wanted so desperately to feel a connection, to feel that glow of happiness. I was going to just look inside, remember the good times, and then leave. Maybe it would help me find some closure.

Inside the dome, the air was hot, humid, and sticky to the point of being uncomfortable. Children in matching T-shirts shrieked through the exhibits, weary looking guardians chasing slowly after them. Some sort of children's tour was going on, filling the room with screaming kids.

I tried to work my way over to the waterfall where Owen and I had eaten our picnic dinner. It looked different in the daylight, the soft glow replaced by the harsh glare of the sun. I could barely hear the musical song of the water falling over the loud screeching of sugar filled kids. I stared at the waterfall for a moment, trying to recall exactly how it had felt the last time I was in this room, but instead of romantic kisses on my lips, strangers kept bumping into me. Everywhere I went, the crowd managed to jostle me.

I remembered the sweet scent of plumeria, and went to find one of the strange-looking trees. I walked around the room, but couldn't find a single one. When I saw a tour guide pointing out various species of edible plants to several interested adults, I headed over and asked where a plumeria tree might be.

"I'm afraid we don't have any plumeria here. I saw one once in Hawaii, though, and they sure are beautiful. Sorry about that," the young woman told me. I sighed, thanked her and headed back to my car.

I was drained. I didn't want to be out anymore. My throat hurt from holding back tears, and I felt shaky and sick. I just wanted to go back to bed. So I hopped in my car, went home, and did exactly that.

***

I woke up early again the next day and immediately got groceries and then hid in my house before the rest of the world could wake up and bother me. I still felt grouchy, and crowds were the last thing I wanted to deal with. I was giving very strong consideration to simply becoming a shut-in and never having to deal with human beings again when Marissa called.

"Hey you! Allie and I are coming to get you at five-thirty to go to Zoo Brew with us, so you'd better be ready," she said into the phone. She had been texting me nonstop from the moment she thought I was awake until well after lunch when she decided to finally just call. There was no doubt in her voice that I was going to go whether I wanted to or not.

"Marissa, I don't know... I mean I'm still jet lagged, and.." I said, trying to get out of it.

"And there is beer and wine at the zoo. Allie and I already bought your ticket. We had such a great time last year when we went, remember? Come on, animals and alcohol? What could be more fun?" I could tell she wasn't going to take no for an answer. Remembering the good time we had dancing to live music and getting free wine samples at the adults only event last year made me smile.

"All right. I'll get dressed and we can go."

"Sweet! We'll come pick you up!" I could hear her grin through the phone. It was hard not to smile back when I thought of how big her smile could be. When I set down the phone, I felt optimistic for the first time all day.

The zoo grounds were hot and humid. It had rained early in the morning, but the sun came out around noon and instead of drying up the water, had just turned the outdoors into a sauna. It wasn't quite to summer levels of heat, but it bordered on uncomfortable. Even the animals looked just a little too warm as we wandered around the zoo, sipping on our plastic cups of wine from the local winery.

I told my two best friends the sterile version of what happened. I had practiced it in the mirror, so I could say it without crying. I had left Dubai because the sheik's son had tried to assault me. Owen and I were broken up. It just wasn't working out. Both women nodded sympathetically, keeping quiet until I changed the subject.

We wandered aimlessly, following the crowd, until we came to an animal enclosure. Adults were playing with the child-sized plastic peep hole, popping their heads up into a bubble in the middle of a prairie dog town.

"I still can't believe you Iowa folks think this counts as a zoo exhibit," Marissa said shaking her head as she peered into the prairie dog exhibit. "Seriously, back home, those things are freaking *everywhere*."

"Yeah, yeah, Ms. New Mexico, but they aren't here. At least I've never seen them," Allie replied. It was a zoo tradition for the three of us to stand here and say these lines. It was comforting to hear them sound exactly the same, like nothing had ever changed.

"It would be like having an exhibit on geese. I'm just tickled pink that you Iowans put them in a zoo." Marissa leaned against the glass as we watched the little rodents scamper in and out of their holes, their high-pitched chirps almost making a song.

"I think I'd like an exhibit of geese," I said as I drank my wine.

"You would," Allie said, shaking her head. I grinned at her. She knew how much I loved walking the river in the spring and looking for baby goslings. It was something I looked forward to every year.

"Let's go look at the tiger. That's at least a *real* animal." Marissa shooed us away from the exhibit, pretending not to glance behind her as we left. Marissa had moved out to Iowa five years ago from New Mexico after a bad breakup, but she still considered New Mexico her home. I knew the prairie dogs were actually her favorite animals here, but that she would never admit it in public.

We dutifully walked toward the tiger enclosure, laughing as we joined a couple watching the tiger. In the big cat's pool, someone had placed what looked like an empty beer keg. The tiger was having the time of his life playing with the giant floating toy. I could see puncture marks through the metal and was glad he was on the other side of the glass.

The tiger crawled out of the water, then turned around and pounced on the floating keg. The keg, of course, bobbed and dunked him into the water with a delightful splash. The tiger popped to the surface a moment later with a look of surprise on his face.

"Aw look, the big kitty made Kaylee smile," Marissa said in a baby voice before she laughed and put her arm around me. I almost punched her, but I knew she was only trying to help me have a good time. The tiger had gotten a hold of the rim of the barrel and was pulling it out of the water, playing with the steel drum like a kitten with a new toy.

"I think he's adorable. You know I've always liked cats," I said nonchalantly. Allie grinned at me. I finished the last of my wine, glad for a moment to feel normal. This was how my life was supposed to be. I loved spending time with my friends, visiting the zoo, and having a good time. For a short minute, I was able to forget that my heart was broken and for that, I loved my friends even more.

"Well, I'm out of wine," I stated, staring into my empty cup. Marissa raised her eyebrows, and Allie shook her head when I didn't move to do anything about it.

"So, go get more. That's the beauty of Zoo Brew. I don't think they've run out of alcohol yet." Marissa pretended to check her watch, making me laugh a little.

"Alright, you two want seconds?"

Allie and Marissa both held out their empty glasses, their eyes back on the tiger.

"Hey! I am not your waitress! This is a self-serve kind of a place ladies," I chastised. They both fell over in a fit of giggles at their supposed cleverness. I shook my head at them, glad to have them in my life. This day was actually becoming enjoyable because of them.

Marissa hooked her arm around mine, and Allie repeated the motion on the other side. "We're off to see the Wizard..." Marissa began to sing, her voice horribly off key.

"Tiger here can be the Cowardly Lion," Allie said, blowing the tiger a kiss as we began walking back toward the wine tent. "I want to be Dorothy. Marissa, you're the Scarecrow."

"Why am I the Scarecrow?" Marissa pouted.

"Because you got no brain, sweetie," Allie said matter-of-factly. I snickered as we turned the bend, walking directly toward the penguin enclosure. My heart stopped as one of the little birds waddled out and dove into the cool water.

"What about Kaylee?" Marissa asked, oblivious to the fact that I had stopped walking and was staring at the black and white birds.

"She's the Tin Man," Allie said softly, following my gaze and understanding immediately, "because she's lost her heart."

Owen tossed a small sardine to one of the penguins, the little bird catching it in it's mouth. Two more hurried up to him, all begging and splashing for the fishy treats. Owen chuckled and handed me the bucket of stinky fish. His eyes were bright with amusement as he watched as the penguins waddle over like I was their new king. He laughed, one of the black and white birds deciding my boot looked like a tasty treat and pecking at it voraciously. They piled on top of one another, their funny bodies wiggling as they asked for more. Owen smiled at me like this was the best day of his life.

My lower lip started to tremble, and tears gathered at the back of my eyes. I could practically see him there, laughing in delight at the funny, flightless birds. They were his favorite animal. A single tear broke through the dam, and suddenly I had buckets of tears pouring down my face. The crack in my heart had finally broken wide, and there was no pretending it was fine now.

Allie and Marissa exchanged a quick glance before practically dragging me off to a park bench hidden behind some trees where we wouldn't be bothered. I couldn't see the penguins anymore, but it didn't matter. The damage was done.

"What have I done? I've lost him," I sobbed into Allie's shoulder. She tucked her chin against my head, holding me to her like a small child as she smoothed my hair. "I should have stayed. I could have stayed and been okay."

"No, honey, you couldn't have." Marissa removed me from Allie's shoulder long enough to make me look at her. "You did the right thing. You couldn't have stayed there."

"But...but.." I couldn't find the words. My nose was running, and I couldn't breathe for crying. Marissa waited until I was calmer before she continued being my voice of reason.

"Kaylee, you did the right thing. You weren't meant to be a part of that desert world. And that's okay. You belong here." She handed me a napkin so I could blow my nose.

"But I love him. I really do."

"I know. Sometimes a fish and a bird fall in love, but that doesn't mean they are going to build a nest and have little fish-bird babies," Marissa said softly. Allie snorted at Marissa's bad analogy, and Marissa gave her a dirty look. "You know what I mean."

A strand of hair fell across my face and Marissa gently tucked it behind my ear with a soft smile. "What's important is that you were happy. I know the 'tis better to have loved and lost' thing is cliché, but it's still true. I know it hurts right now, but it's going to be okay."

I looked at her, tears still streaming down my face. I felt so lost, even with my friends on either side of me. Marissa sighed. "I can throw some more cliches at you if it will help you feel better."

I knew she was hoping to get a smile out of me, but I couldn't find one to give. Allie gave me a squeeze.

"It sucks right now. And it's gonna suck for a while. It *will* get better though. You'll get your happy ending someday, I promise." Allie gave me a hug. I knew they were trying their best, but there were no magic words that could fill the hole in my heart. I wished to heaven there were, but I knew it was just going to take time.

"I'm going to go get you some more wine. I think you can use some drunk time," Marissa said, putting a hand on my shoulder as she stood. She gave me a squeeze and headed off in the direction of the wine tent. I leaned my head back against Allie's shoulder, her blonde hair mixing with mine.

"After this, we'll head back to my place and drink crappy wine, watch crappy movies, and eat good ice cream. Okay?" Allie kept smoothing my hair with her hands, and I closed my eyes to her soothing touch.

"No skimping on the ice cream."

I felt her smile as she looked down at me. "I would never even dream of such a thing."

I sat up, remembering all the cleaning and baking I had done. There was no way I was going to eat all those cookies myself. "How about we do it at my place? It's actually clean for once."

Allie nodded and let me put my head back on her shoulder. She resumed gently stroking my hair as she whispered, "Sure, Kaylee, anything you want."

CHAPTER TWENTY-ONE

My head buzzed as I sat up, the room unfamiliar. Slowly, I realized I had fallen asleep on the floor in front of the TV. The menu of a DVD was on loop, the instrumental song starting over every twenty seconds. I hit the power button, the pain in my head decreasing as the annoying song went away.

I glanced at my watch, glad to see it was a little past ten instead of hours before dawn. Maybe my jet lag was finally wearing off. Marissa was snoring peacefully on the couch, the slight wheeze and chuckle rather endearing. I looked around for Allie, finally finding her curled up in the papasan chair, a blanket draped over her head. I smiled at my friends, then frowned as I looked around at the mess they had made.

Pizza boxes littered the floor, empty beer cans

hiding among them. Three empty wine glasses sat on the coffee table, a row of shot glasses lined up neatly beside them. How the shot glasses got there was a complete mystery to me, but I was sure I would hear about it once the girls woke up.

I picked up the pizza boxes, stacking them in a pile by the door. I went to my room and threw on the first pants I found, and a light blue shirt. I stepped outside, humidity hitting me in the face like a wet towel. I was glad I had good air conditioning in my apartment. It was already hot and muggy, the sky threatening to burst at any time.

Back inside, Allie and Marissa were up and putting the glasses in the dishwasher, moving slowly but nonetheless getting things done. Allie gave me a big grin as I came back inside, then she grabbed her stomach and looked a little green. Marissa laughed at her, but the motion made her grab her bright red hair and grimace.

"I think the shots might have been a mistake," she groaned.

"No kidding. How are you up and moving around, Kaylee? You were slamming them back as fast as we were," Allie groaned, closing the dishwasher. I opened the fridge and gave them each a sports drink.

"I guess I just hold my liquor better than the two of you. I don't remember doing shots, though," I answered.

"That's because you didn't. You were passed out on the floor when *someone* decided it was a good idea." Marissa took a big sip of her drink and leaned against the counter, glaring at Allie.

Allie blushed. "I guess I really overdid it if I didn't realize Kaylee wasn't drinking hers. No wonder I feel it today."

"You two look like you might pass out or barf any minute now. Go sit on the couch and relax. I'll get the rest of this. You guys took care of me last night. I can take care of you this morning." I shooed them toward the couch, but Marissa stopped me.

"Honestly, I just want a shower and to crawl into my own bed. Thank you, Kaylee, but I'm going to head home. Besides, your shampoo sucks." Marissa gave me a weak smile to show she wasn't trying to be mean.

"I'm with you on the going home," Allie said quietly, holding her stomach like it might fall out if she let go. "Thanks for the offer, Kaylee, but I want to be miserable in my own bed."

"All right. How about I bring you two soup later then? It's the least I can do," I said, helping them gather the last of their things.

"That sounds fantastic. Make that chicken dumpling one for me?" Allie asked, seeming to perk up a little bit. I nodded and promised as the two of them staggered zombie like down the hall. They were going to need a lot more than soup to make those hangovers better.

Back inside my own apartment, I cleaned up the last of our sleepover and organized the kitchen. It wasn't long before my phone chirped with a message from Allie that they had both made it home safe and sound.

I played with the phone in my hand, toying with the idea of sending a message to Owen. I opened a message three times, stared at the blank page with no idea what to say, only to close it again. What could I possibly say to Owen that would make this better? I just had to deal with the fact that there was no easy way to fix this. Owen was gone.

Thunder rumbled outside, making my neighbor's dog bark. Technically the building didn't allow dogs, but somehow the dog was still there. I knew Emma would know how to calm the dog down from the storm. I smiled at the thought of my sister, then looked down at the phone. I was already on my speed dial page, my thumb poised over her number.

"Hey, Kaylee, how're you doing?" Emma's voice was music to my ears. I should have called her first thing when I got back instead of waiting this long.

"Crappy. I assume you've heard all about it," I said, settling into the couch.

"Yeah, but I'd rather hear it from you. I just had a meeting cancel on me, so I've got some spare time." I could just see her in my head, spinning around in an office chair and smiling at the phone.

I started by telling her about Dubai, the skyscrapers and the hotel, then the dinner at the sheik's house. I told her how uncomfortable the sheik's son made me, how he leered and made my skin crawl.

"I should have known something was off about Roger, but I thought he was harmless. Creepy, but harmless." I sighed. "The next day he got in my hotel room, Emma. He just walked right in like it was nothing."

"I heard about that. I'm glad Dean got there in time. I'm so sorry this happened to you," Emma said softly. I didn't trust my voice to answer right away.

"Emma, it's all so messed up. I told Owen that we can't be together. His life is in Dubai and I won't, I can't, ever go back there. That fucking prick messed everything up." I was surprised at my own anger, especially since I almost never cussed, but it felt good to call him a name.

"Well, I can completely understand why Owen told the sheik off about it. What his son did was completely inappropriate."

"What do you mean, 'Owen told the sheik off?'" I asked confused.

"You mean he didn't tell you? It's all Jack's been able to talk about for the past few days. Owen went completely berserk on him."

As Emma told me what happened, I could see it all clearly in my head.

CHAPTER TWENTY-TWO

Owen clicked the phone shut. If he could have slammed the receiver down like on an old corded phone, he would have. His hands shook as he held the phone in disbelief. He'd heard news reports of how Western ex-pats had been mistreated in Dubai, but nothing like this. He walked out of the private room where he had excused himself to talk to Dean, intent on giving the sheik one chance to make this right. One chance.

In another moment, he was back at the negotiation table with the sheik. Owen's usual poker face was gone, and the sheik noticed immediately. "Is something wrong?"

"Yeah, something's wrong alright. Your son just tried to assault my girlfriend," Owen said.

A flash of anger crossed the older man's face for

a moment before it softened again. Anger at his son's actions, Owen hoped. "That's a serious accusation, Mr. Parker. An accusation that you shouldn't make lightly."

"I'm serious as a heart attack right now. I have two witnesses, and probably the room service guy as well. What are you going to do about this?" Owen's eyes burned like fire.

al-Saffar shrugged his shoulders. "I'm sure the hotel staff will be more than happy to tell us what really happened later tonight. In the meantime, let's get back to the negotiations."

Owen slammed his hand against the table. "We'll be dealing with this right now, before you have a chance to get the hotel staff to change their stories, or these negotiations are over."

The sheik turned red, practically shaking with barely contained rage. "I'm not sure I appreciate your tone, Mr. Parker."

Owen stood up, walking to the window. The Burj Khalifa gleamed in the distance, a sand storm preparing to engulf it from behind. "It's a beautiful sight, the tower. The tallest structure in the world. The crown jewel of Dubai."

"Please, let's just return to negotiations for now? We can talk about this later," al-Saffar said.

"But it wasn't able to be completed by just Dubai," Owen continued, looking out the window. "Dubai ran out of money and needed to be bailed out by the United Arab Emirates, and so what was supposed to be the Burj Dubai was renamed the Burj Khalifa to honor the Khalifa family for their

support."

Sheik al Saffar remained silent. This was a sore spot for all of Dubai, and both men knew it.

"But I'm not sure 'Burj Khalifa' is the right name for it either. I think that you owe way too much to the West and that it's time you recognized that. I was thinking, maybe you should rename it the 'Burj British Petroleum'. Or maybe 'Wells Fargo Tower'."

"How dare you..." the sheik said from behind him.

Owen cut him off. "Or, you know, maybe just convert it to a Marriott hotel. Either that or just let Wal-Mart buy the whole thing; I'm sure their sign would look great on the 150th floor."

"Listen here..." the sheik started.

"No, you listen here," Owen said, his voice rising as he turned around. His finger shot out, pointing straight at the older man. "I've noticed your son flirting with Kaylee, and I've noticed the looks he gives her when he thinks she's not looking. You either get him under control, or these negotiations are over."

al Saffar jumped to his feet, his own voice roaring. "I think you've forgotten who you're talking to, Mr. Parker. I think you've forgotten that your name isn't Daniel Saunders."

Owen laughed. "Perhaps you haven't heard, but the owner's name is Jack now." He walked to the table and picked up his briefcase. "These negotiations are over. Either call me when you've come to your senses and have your son under control, or call Saunders and let him know that the deal is off." He walked toward the door.

"You have no right-" the sheik yelled after him, cut off by the sound of the door slamming behind Owen.

***

"He really did that?" I asked, flabbergasted. I knew Owen had been angry, but I had no idea that he would go to those lengths.

"Yeah. The sheik was pissed. He woke Jack up at 3 in the morning to tell him what Owen did."

"What did Jack do?" I hoped that Owen wasn't going to get in too much trouble over this, but I had a feeling that this wasn't going to end well.

"Well, Jack was furious at first. This could ruin years of business negotiations. Billions of dollars lost. I've never seen Jack that angry." Emma paused for a moment before continuing. "But when he calmed down enough to think straight, he realized he would have done the same thing in Owen's position."

"What's going to happen to Owen?" I asked, breathless.

"I'm not sure. The sheik demanded Owen's immediate dismissal, but I don't know how Jack is going to take that. Owen and Jack have been locked in Jack's office for the past two days. I haven't even been able to bring Jack his hamburger today." I could practically hear Emma shrug her shoulders. "I wish I could tell you what's going to happen, but I don't have a clue myself."

"Will you let me know if anything happens?"

"Sure, but won't Owen tell you first?"

"Um, well, we haven't talked since I got back to Iowa," I said quietly.

"What? Not even a text?" Emma was shocked. I knew her eyes would be wide open and her mouth would hang open just a little.

"I told him we couldn't be together. I wish I would have known that he had confronted the sheik though." I leaned my head back and looked up at the ceiling, trying to figure out what I should do. I couldn't think of a good answer.

"Oh, KayKay," Emma said with a sigh. "I'll tell him to call you next time I see him. I've gotta go back to work now. Are you going to be okay?"

I grimaced and rubbed my eyes, emotions tumbling around inside of me. "Yeah, I'll be fine. Thanks for talking to me."

"Anytime. I'll give you a call tomorrow, okay? Love you!"

"Love you too, Emma." I hung up the phone and just stared at it in my hand.

Wave after wave of emotions washed through me, each one pummeling the one before it until I wasn't sure what I felt anymore. Awe that he had stood up for me like that. Love because he would risk so much. Anger that he hadn't told me. Fear for what would happen to him. Despair that he was gone. Hopelessness for what would never be.

I lay down on the couch, curling up into a tight ball. I didn't know what else to do, so I just closed my eyes and prayed for sleep.

CHAPTER TWENTY-THREE

I awoke with a start, nearly falling off the couch as the front door buzzed. I hadn't meant to doze off and the afternoon crept up on me. I rubbed the sleep out of my eyes, glancing out the window. It was raining again, the room bathed in a gray light. The intercom buzzed again and I got up to answer it.

I hit 'answer' only to be met with static. *Right*, I remembered, t*he buzzer's broken. Have to go down and answer it in person.* I pulled my hair up into a messy ponytail, not even bothering to put on shoes for the quick trip down the stairs.

I hurried down and pushed open the locked main entrance door, not expecting the wind to rush out of my body and my heart to jump in my chest.

Owen stood in the entrance. He was wearing just simple jeans and a white button-up short-sleeved shirt, but he looked like a knight in shining armor to me. He gave me a crooked smile as I opened the door.

"Hi, Kaylee," he greeted me, running a hand through his rain soaked hair. Little droplets of water went flying, sparkling like diamonds as they fell.

"What are you doing here?" I gasped in amazement. I was sure he was going to disappear at any moment, that I was going to wake up and be back in my bed alone.

"I told you that I'd be back. I just had some things I needed to do first." His smile lit up my world. I took a step forward, afraid he would shimmer and fade like a desert mirage. He stepped forward and took my hands in his. They were wet from the rain, but still warm and strong.

"There's something I need to tell you, Kaylee." His blue eyes searched my face, their crystalline depths holding me captive. "I quit my job."

"What? Why would you do that?" I asked in surprise. He smiled down at me and brushed a tendril of hair from my face.

"Because it wasn't making me happy anymore. *You* make me happy. I couldn't bear the thought of taking another trip without you."

I pulled back slightly in surprise. "But you love your job!"

"No, I love the *challenge* of my job. The job itself is immaterial. Without you, it wasn't fun anymore. When I was away from you, all I did was miss you. I don't want the job anymore. I just want you." He said it simply, as though it were nothing but fact, but it made my heart pound in my chest.

"What about the sheik? And Jack?"

"Oh, you heard about that?" Owen flushed slightly as he shrugged. "Publicly, Jack is going to fire me. Privately, I quit. It saves face for Jack and the company, the sheik gets what he wants, and I get what I want.

You."

I opened my mouth, but couldn't find any words. No one had ever made me as happy as Owen did with that one small word: *You*. He wanted only me.

"There is one down side, though," he said, giving me a thoughtful look. "It does mean that we will have to be slightly frugal. I won't have the paychecks from Jack's company rolling in anymore."

"I'll pick up extra shifts at the hospital," I said, only half-joking. I would do whatever it took. I wasn't letting go of him ever again.

Owen laughed and pulled me closer. "Not that frugal! I still have a stake in the company, but we should probably just borrow Jack's private jet instead of buying our own."

"That's fine by me. I hate flying anyway." I could feel a silly grin spreading across my face, happiness bubbling up inside of me.

"In the meantime, though, I am going to need a job. I was wondering if you were still interested in opening that bed and breakfast. Maybe even having some help from your husband?" he asked.

My mouth dropped open. "Is this some kind of proposal?" I asked.

Owen leaned down, not answering the question. His hair dripped rainwater onto my face as he kissed me softly. My heart soared in my chest, every fiber of my being taking flight. Owen was mine and I was his. We didn't have to be apart anymore. "Yes," I said, not waiting for him to repeat the question. "A thousand times yes." I leaned back in and kissed him again.

Owen broke the kiss, and smiled down at me. "Jack and Emma met on vacation. *You* are my vacation. You are the person that makes me feel relaxed and wonderful. Wherever you are is home to me."

I reached up and touched his cheek, losing myself in his cobalt eyes. "I love you, Owen Parker."

"I love you, Kaylee LaRue."

And then he kissed me.

❧❧❧❧

EPILOGUE

I stand anxious at the back of the church, smoothing the satin of my dress with sweaty palms. I'm not anxious about what I am doing; I'm anxious that I am going to trip or stutter in front of all these people. I was meant to be with him, and this ceremony is just to show the world what we already know. There is no anxiety about what I am doing when it comes to Owen.

The organ music starts, filling the church with a beautiful melody. I hold my bouquet of plumeria to my nose and inhale the delicate flowers once more. These flowers are Owen's and mine. They represent our love. Beautiful and sweet. I smile, and step through the ornate wooden doors.

Mom and Dad walk on either side of me, the two of them beaming with pride as we move in time with the music. Mom is crying, but she keeps dabbing a Kleenex to her eyes so her mascara doesn't run. Dad's lips are tight, but it's to keep them from quivering as he walks his oldest daughter down the aisle. I know they're proud of me.

Everything disappears. I don't see anything or anyone but Owen. The old church with its intricate stained-glass windows, the pews with red satin seats, the bridesmaids and the groomsmen, they all just seem to fade away. The only person that matters is standing there, grinning, waiting for me to join him.

I kiss my parents, whispering that I love them as they let me go. Dad shakes Owen's hand and claps him on the shoulder. I know I'm blushing as Owen reaches out his hand to help me up onto the dais. Owen's hands are as clammy as mine, and we grin at one another. I'm happier right now than I ever thought possible. In this moment, everything is perfect.

The minister begins speaking, but I'm not looking at him. I'm looking at the man I'm marrying, the man who holds the key to my heart. I glance out at the people watching us, noticing them for the first time, and seeing only smiles and tears of joy.

I can see my sister from the corner of my eye, smiling as a tear runs down her cheek. She doesn't bother wiping it away, unashamed at her joy. Marissa and Allie stand behind her, the two of them grinning like this is the best day of their lives. I know it certainly is for me.

The minister asks Owen a question, and he looks at me with eyes more blue than I've ever seen. "I do," he says, his voice shaking with emotion but full of confidence. Jack hands him a ring, and Owen carefully slides the stone onto my left hand. It sparkles in the light, full of hope and promise.

The minister turns to me, and I make the same promise, Emma handing me a platinum man's ring. Owen mouths, "I love you," as I slip it on his finger. I smile and almost kiss him right there, but catch myself just in time.

I lose myself in Owen's eyes, surprised when I finally hear the words I've been waiting my whole life to hear. Owen grins, happiness radiating out of him as he reaches for me and our lips meet. I can hear people cheering, but it's nothing compared to the joy inside my head.

I capture this moment in my mind, treasuring every detail like a precious jewel. Someday, I will tell my grandchildren of this moment and how, even though we were indoors, it tasted like rainwater kisses.

RAINWATER KISSES

ABOUT THE AUTHOR

Krista Lakes is a mother who recently rediscovered her passion for writing. She loves aquatic life and running marathons. She is living happily ever after with her Prince Charming and her two crazy (but wonderful) kids.

Krista would love to hear from you! Please contact her at Krista.Lakes@gmail.com or like her on Facebook!